Legacy of Kane

"Let your imagination become a gateway to a whole other world."

Timothy Aberle

• Chicago •

Legacy of Kane
Timothy Aberle

Published by
Joshua Tree Publishing
• Chicago •
JoshuaTreePublishing.com

13-Digit ISBN: 978-1-941049-93-8

Illustrations: Catya Elise

Disclaimer:

Printed in the United States of America

Dedication

This book is dedicated to my father Heinrich Aberle. Through your life accomplishments and ambitious motivation, you've built a legacy that will forever cement the Aberle family's place in the world. Because of you, our family looks to a bright future.

Table of Contents

Preface:
The End Is The Beginning

Danika

They say every beginning has an end. What if I told you—the end is the beginning. Something old replaced with something new. Such is the story of the fall of my ancestor Jesus and the reckoning of heaven.

As a child, I learned everything I could about the entries stored within the elder grimoire. My father always told me, "Knowledge is key, and without it we would cease to be." He told me that one day I would turn to the entries in the grimoire for guidance and answers and in time insert entries of my own. I always wondered what my first entry in the grimoire would be.

The entries started long before the fall of heaven and the rise of the dark lord. Reading the grimoire was much like reading a novel or someone's diary. It chronicled my family's origin—everything from beautiful, blissful moments to mass-evil, chaotic times. I had learned many fascinating things about my family through its teachings and loved the adventures I found in some of the entries. My favorite entries were those written of my grandparents Nathaniel and Everin.

I read that my grandfather Nathaniel was a very brave and wise angel. He was best known by all for his quick wit, erudition, and teaching skills. My father learned everything from Nathaniel. But like any being, Nathaniel had flaws. His family meant the world to him so much that he kept many secrets and truths from them. In doing so, he caused much heartache and pain to those he loved most. But his biggest secret was the one he kept closest to his heart: his endless, pure love for Everin Goodwater, the daughter of God, the most beautiful angel in all existence. Nathaniel wrote in an entry that Everin's last words were, "Nathaniel, the babies . . ." It's sad to think that Nathaniel lived for so long and never knew till the end of his time that Jensen and Rayne were his children, offspring of the time he and Everin spent together and the love they shared. The entries written by Everin, I found to be legendary, and the legacy she left was hope. I revered her for her strength, but questions lingered on my mind about her last entry. She said that she had felt the coldness of the dark lord around her and that she felt her time would be over soon. When she took her last breath and heaven fell to darkness, it was 3:15 a.m. The significance of 3:15 a.m. has remained in question as it was the time Everin was born and the time she died. Jesus was born at 3:15 a.m., and thirty-three years later, he took his last breath. At that same time, my father was born at 3:15 a.m., as was I.

I read that when Nathaniel found Everin dying, the grimoire was on the ground next to her, covered in her blood. Through her blood, the grimoire recorded her last hours. "The Battered Angel" was the entry title, and at the very end of the entry, signed in Everin's blood, it read: "The end is just the beginning."

The Battered Angel

Everin

The clock stopped at 3:15. The sheer bright light was heaven's reckoning, and the shallow concussions that followed were heaven's last breaths. This place was once full of life, love, and luster until the dark and turbulent times began. I watched as my fellow angels and souls fell into the grip of madness, and some embraced the chaos that surrounded them. Darkness was everywhere, and livestock were slaughtered for amusement by the jinn. This was the time that the great evil happened and deranged chanting was heard as the jinn set fire to my Father's most divine ridges. Our beautiful paradise became empty and hollow as evil scattered across heaven. In these dark times, all I could think about was seeing Nathaniel's face again.

When I was dragged away into the spiderweb of darkness, I felt the pin prick, and I knew the jinn had injected me with some kind of poisonous toxin. As the minutes passed, the toxin entered my bloodstream like liquid fire. Coursing through my veins, it infected my body vigorously. This weakened my ability to fight, heal, and call upon the Nevillin. Each time I flicked my wrist, the Nevillin would not appear. Looking at the jinn, I could see that they yearned to kill me. *But what held them back?* They knew I'd be vulnerable to their weapons and violence.

They took me to a cell unfamiliar to me. I knew whatever this was constructed with was something of pure evil. The bars of the cell were something out of a horror movie as they were coated with flesh of angels. I saw feathers that remained of whatever horror might have taken place there. The only light in the cell was that of the moon as it shone down through a small barred window. Remaining calm, I sat in the middle of the cell and meditated on what was to come. Then I heard a woman and her children scream. Looking through the bars, I saw two jinn dragging and pulling the soul of a woman and her two children apart, throwing the children in one cell and the woman in the one next to me. She fell to her knees and began to pray.

"It's no use," I said, shaking my head. "My Father can't hear your prayers anymore."

"Princess Everin," she said, happy to see me, "what are you doing here?"

"Same as you," I said, looking at her.

"You were captured?" she asked surprised. "I thought the Elders held godlike powers?" she asked before touching my hand. "Fazin," she said quietly, "the drug is related to Marafol."

"Marafol? How do you know this?" I demanded as two jinn unlocked my cell. "How do you know this?" I shouted at her frustrated.

"Silence, you!" one of the jinn sneered as it came into the cell to escort me out.

As I was being walked down a long, narrow corridor, I could feel the Fazin wearing off, and I was able to get the upper hand. I hit them both using my wings and got them off me. Though I was unable to call on the Nevillin, I found the strength to take flight. Bursting out through the ceiling of this dark place, I saw that I had never even left heaven. It was dark, raining, and windy, and everywhere in heaven was covered in evil. I looked and saw that my Father's once-beautiful and once-beloved ocean had become dark and restless. As I looked at the fires and carnage taking place, I closed my eyes and heard Nathaniel's voice in my head: *"Everin, it's a mistake to harness that much evil in one place. Creating the abyss is a mistake."*

I saw what remained of the elders still fighting the jinn. I saw Lucifer, Nathaniel, and Maya. I saw fire and black smoke coming out from all the windows of my Father's home. Flying over to the balcony where our inauguration took place, I crept inside and made my way through the hallways and up the staircase to my Father's chamber. There I saw two jinn trying to break down the door. The hallway to the door was very high, so I quietly took flight and hovered above the jinn to sneak up on them. In one swift motion, I flew down like a bullet, taking them out as quietly as possible, snapping their necks. Turning around, I saw three more jinn coming at me. Then suddenly, out of nowhere, they were taken out by an entity whose face was shadowed by the hood of a dark cloak.

"Who are you?" I demanded from the entity.

"It's me," it said in a deep voice, unveiling itself.

"Roquin?" I said confused. "What happened to you? We thought you were dead."

"What are you still doing here, Everin?" Roquin asked as I opened the door to the chamber and walked in.

"You know I can't leave without the holy relics," I said, flicking my wrist. The Nevillin did not appear. "How did you survive, Roquin?" I asked carefully as his back was turned to me, and he looked at me through the corner of his eye as I collected the relics into a brown satchel.

"Like you, I fought hard to get back here," he said.

"Like me?" I asked confused.

"You know, when you were dragged into the darkness," he said as I backed away from him.

"How do you know about that?" I asked curiously. "That happened after we thought you died," I said, grabbing the last of the relics.

"No, it didn't," he said, looking at me.

"How did you survive, Roquin?" I asked as he continued to look at me and shake his head. "I knew it," I said, flicking my wrist again, and the Nevillin finally appeared.

"Fazin really doesn't last as long as we'd like it to," Roquin said anxiously before flicking his wrist.

"It was you!" I shouted in shock, pointing the Nevillin at him. "Deceiver!"

"I had no choice, Everin," Roquin pleaded.

"We all have choices, Roquin," I said, upset and feeling betrayed.

"If you'd only listen to me . . ."

"No!" I shouted scared. "I don't want to hear your lies!"

"See, that's what I thought too, until I, too, was told the secrets God hid from us," Roquin said, trying to justify his betrayal.

"Give me the relics, Everin."

"You're not in this alone?" I asked surprised.

"Clever girl," Roquin said as he smiled sinisterly.

"You should be ashamed of yourself," I said in disgust.

"Pot calling the kettle black. You had no issue lusting for an elder that didn't belong to you, but I should be ashamed?" Roquin said, shaking his head. "You're as bad as me. What did the two of you talk about while in bed together? Better yet . . . tell me, does Nathaniel know his offspring lie in your womb?" Roquin asked, looking at me sinisterly. "Give me the relics, Everin," Roquin demanded, grinding his teeth, "and I can fix everything. I'll make everything back the way it was, when God loved us most."

"No," I said as Roquin swung his katana and I blocked it.

Taking off as fast as I could, I flew through the air and ripped through all the jinn in my path. I saw Maya fly into the sky, breaking the sound barrier, while Nathaniel and Lucifer fought jinn off them. I flew in all different directions until Maya came down from the sky, breaking through heaven's crust. I flew to where she'd broken through, knowing my time was limited to when the opening in the crust would close. I flew faster than I ever did. Seeing the opening, I threw the bag of relics in after her. When I saw that one of the three Trivium blades didn't make it into the opening, I went for it, but before I could get to it, something hit me out of the sky. Crashing through the side of my Father's home and coming to a stop by the entryway door, I picked my head up and looked around when suddenly I was kicked in the face.

"Oh, Everin, to think there was a time I lusted for you," Roquin said, grabbing my face and forcing me to look at him as he injected me with another vial of Fazin. "I'd watch you day in and day out, not that you'd ever notice me. I would've done anything for you," Roquin said, pacing in front of me. "Till one night, at one of our ridiculous gatherings, I saw you sneak away with Nathaniel. I watched as you and he made love, for a moment I even envied him. But as I looked at the both of you, I could tell that your affair was something that had been going on for a very long time. Then I was struck with rage."

"So you did this out of jealousy?" I asked as I spit up a mouthful of blood and gasped in pain.

"I did at first. But then it turned into something else," Roquin explained.

"And what might that have been?" I asked, before he jumped on top of me and began punching me in the face repeatedly until my face was swollen and my body became limp.

"I knew if I couldn't have you, neither could he," he said.

Ripping the armor and clothes from my body till I was nude, he grabbed at my flesh wherever he could. When I resisted, he began punching me in the stomach and ribs. When the jinn arrived, he instructed them to tie my hands and feet with rope. Spreading my nude body open, the four jinn held the ropes as Roquin invaded me. Like an animal, he bit my breasts and nipples so hard that immediately bruising and bleeding occurred. Picking my head up, I bit his nipple and ripped a chunk out of him.

"Ahhh!" he shouted in pain. "Give me the rope," he demanded from one of the jinn.

Putting it around my neck, he instructed the jinn to pull it tight. As I gasped for air, Roquin bit my left breast at the nipple and tore my flesh.

"Playtime's over, my dear," he said as he showed me the Trivium blade that had missed the opening. "Drop something?" he asked before he drove the blade into the lower part of my stomach, cutting me open. Reaching inside, he took one of the babies out and cut its umbilical cord. It was crying aloud, and he handed it to one of the jinn before reaching in one last time to pull out the last one.

"Know this, Princess, your children will know nothing other than a world of torment and evil," Roquin said as I tried to talk while choking on blood.

"What's that? What are you saying?" Roquin mocked as the Trivium blade disappeared.

"She said, 'Look behind you,'" a female voice said.

"Who the hell are you?" Roquin asked, demanding an answer.

"The beginning of the end," she said, stripping the baby away from Roquin and kicking him to the ground, before she was attacked by a horde of jinn.

Blocking the jinn's attacks with her katana, Roquin saw Nathaniel enter the room and vanished with the other child.

There in the entryway of God's home lay a broken, battered angel, beautiful white wings stained in blood, with the elder grimoire lying beside her that recorded the last couple of hours of her life.

Legacy at Birth

In snow-covered Bethlehem, there were white caps everywhere I looked. It had to have been the worst storm in Bethlehem's history. It was cold and dark when I, Joseph rode into town on a carriage being towed by two horses accompanied by my wife, Mary. The only light we had was two old lanterns Mary had gotten from her cousin Elizabeth before we'd set out on our journey.

"It's too far, Joseph," Mary said, crying from birthing pains. "We won't make it."

"We will, it's just a little further," I said calmly, taking Mary's hand. "You'll see, we're almost there."

"We can't see anything other than what's right in front of us," Mary said. "It's hopeless."

"Look, Mary, a shooting star," I said when a bright light began falling from the sky. The light was so brilliant that it pierced through the storm and lit up the town of Bethlehem and the road we were on. "It's a sign from God. He's lighting the way for us," I said as I pushed the horses to ride faster toward Bethlehem.

Riding into town, I went to the first inn I saw. I jumped off the carriage and quickly tied up the horses and knocked on the door; it was then that the storm became worse, and it began to hail.

"Yes," a man said, opening the door.

"Do you have any rooms available?" I asked politely.

"Where's that light coming from?" the man asked distracted, looking out the open door.

"It's a falling star," I said as the man looked.

"I apologize," the man said. "I have no rooms available," he said, shutting the door before I put my hand up to stop it.

"Please, there must be something you can do, my wife is with child, and we've traveled very far to get here."

"I'm sorry, I can't help," the man said before hearing Mary cry out, and his conscience came into play.

"Joseph, the pains are really bad!" Mary cried.

The man at the door heard and felt horrible.

"I have a *kataluma*. It's not much, but it's shelter," the man said as the light outside dimmed.

"Thank you so much, that would be fine," I said as Mary took a step to get off the carriage and looked up at the sky.

"I don't think that's a falling star," she whispered as I helped her down.

"Luke, who are these people?" a lady asked, walking into the *kataluma*.

"They're guests seeking shelter," Luke said. "This is my wife, Anne," Luke said to us, introducing her to Mary and I. "Anne, would you please grab blankets and lay them out on the floor please?"

"I'll be right back," Anne said, taking a deep breath and looking at Mary before walking away.

"How far have you traveled?" Luke asked, looking at me.

"From Jerusalem," I said.

"Jerusalem?" Luke repeated deep in thought. "You're on the run from King Herod's issued census, aren't you?"

"We are," I said, looking at Luke, questioning his motives.

"They say King Herod appointed his chief priests and scribes to find someone, a child known as the Messiah. They were given strict orders that once he is found, they are to report his whereabouts so that the king may come to pay homage and worship the child."

"Herod intends to murder the Messiah," I said, holding the handle of my sword.

"I heard about the murders of innocent children and babies," Luke said saddened. "I also heard of many that were murdered by his own hand."

"Mary, you carry the Messiah," Anne said, walking over to

her. "Its birth is a blessing to the world," Anne said, smiling and then looking at Luke and me. "Please lie down, we must see that it is delivered into the world safely."

"What is your name?" Luke asked, putting his hand out to shake mine.

"Joseph Christ. You?" I asked.

"Luke Avengist."

"How is it that your wife knows about the Messiah?" I asked.

"Because I told her," a man said, walking into the *kataluma*.

"I knew that wasn't a falling star," Mary said, smiling. "Nathaniel."

"Who are you?" Luke asked, looking at Nathaniel.

"He is the elder angel Nathaniel," Anne said.

"Elder angel," Luke said, thinking.

"Who do you think showed you the dream that you'd deliver the Messiah into the world, Luke?" Nathaniel asked, putting his hand on Luke's shoulder.

"But . . . that was a dream," Luke said.

"Just a dream, you sure about that?" Nathaniel asked, smiling. "God chose you and Anne to see the Messiah into the world safely."

"Chose!" Luke said frightened.

"You're a gifted surgeon, Luke," Nathaniel said.

"The last baby I tried to deliver . . . ," Luke paused, "things went wrong."

"But nonetheless, you saved her," Nathaniel said, putting his arm around Luke. "That child is still alive today because of you. It's time you stop living in the past and see the Messiah delivered into the world."

"Is the pain supposed to feel like this?" Mary said, scrunching after getting sharp pains.

"What does it feel like?" Luke asked.

"Death," Mary said as blood began to cover the blankets.

"This is your time, Luke," Nathaniel said, looking into Luke's eyes. "See it done."

"All right," Luke said, taking a deep breath. "I need more blankets and a bowl of water," Luke said as Anne assisted him.

"There's something wrong," Luke said, placing his hand on Mary's stomach. "The umbilical cord is around the baby's neck."

"Am I going to lose my baby?" Mary cried as I looked on in fear.

"Mary, look at me," Nathaniel said as she became calm and looked into his eyes. "Everything is going to be fine, I promise," Nathaniel said, looking at Mary as I brought a bowl of water to Luke.

"Is everything okay?" I asked.

"Everything is fine, Joseph. Come over here and be with your wife," Nathaniel said calmly.

"Mary, you need to push," Luke said softly, helping push on her stomach to guide the baby out. "Push, Mary," Luke said as Nathaniel gently placed his hand on her stomach.

Blue light began glowing in between his hand and her stomach as I held her hand, praying.

"There he is," Luke said, smiling and laughing with joy as the baby cried. "It's a boy."

"He's beautiful, Mary. Congratulations!" Anne said, holding him. "Here is your beautiful son," Anne said as she handed the baby to Mary.

"Enreal," Nathaniel whispered.

"What's Enreal?" I asked.

"It's his name in angelic scripture. It means 'savior.'"

"We're going to call you Jesus," Mary said, looking at him.

"That's a beautiful name," Nathaniel said as there was a knock at the door.

"May I help you?" I asked, answering the door.

"Joseph, no!" Nathaniel shouted before I felt a knife stab me in the stomach.

Nathaniel quickly ran at my attacker, kicking him out the door into the street. Then another came at Nathaniel with a crossbow, shooting an arrow at Nathaniel. Nathaniel caught the arrow and snapped it with one hand. Walking up to the attacker, Nathaniel grabbed him by the throat and threw him to the ground, holding him there.

"Joseph, can you stand?" Nathaniel asked calmly, turning his head to look at me.

"I think so," I said in a shallow breath, holding my stomach and coughing.

"Get your son and hold him," Nathaniel said. "Do it now."

"How bad is it, Luke?" I asked as Luke looked at the wound and Anne gave me Jesus to hold.

"It's deep," Luke said as I coughed up blood.

"Here, take this, apply pressure," Luke said, handing me a towel and walking over to Nathaniel.

"Joseph," Mary said.

"I know," I said, looking at Jesus.

"Who are they?" Luke asked, looking at the two men on the ground.

"Scribes of Herod," Nathaniel said, looking at the backs of their necks that had a tattoo that represented Herod.

"I've never seen anything like that before," Luke said, looking at the tattoo of a triangle with an *H* in the middle.

"Come help me drag them inside," Nathaniel said as Luke helped. "Lay him here next to the other."

"Joseph, don't close your eyes," Mary said as I began to collapse in my chair, still holding Jesus, before Nathaniel walked over and held me up.

"Is this your daddy, Jesus?" Nathaniel said, holding me up and looking at Jesus. "Can you show Daddy how much you love him?"

Suddenly a brilliant bright white light between Jesus and I radiated, and my wound was healed as if it never happened.

"My son," I said, looking at Jesus before hugging him.

"That's not all your son can do," Nathaniel said and smiled. "Bring him here," Nathaniel said, kneeling down next to one of the scribes that were knocked out. "Place Jesus's hand on the scribe's face."

"What will that do?" I asked as Nathaniel looked at me and smiled.

"Luke, Anne, come and witness the miracle that is Jesus," Nathaniel said as I placed Jesus's hand on the scribe as instructed.

"My Lord," one of the scribes said, seeing Jesus's hand on them.

"The Messiah," the other scribe said. "Praise the Lord, the Savior is born."

"Come, my friends, today you are reborn, and your new king shows mercy to those who repent," Nathaniel said as there was another knock at the door.

"Allow me," Nathaniel insisted, walking over to the door.

"Greetings. Where might we find the one who has been born king of the Jews?" one of the men asked when Nathaniel opened the door. "We saw his star and have traveled from Yemen to worship him."

"You are very welcome here," Nathaniel said as he invited them to come and see Jesus.

"Followed the star?" Luke asked.

"The bright star that lit the sky was prophesied by this elder angel," one of the three kings spoke and explained. "'On the night of his birth, you will see the brightest star, which will signify God's presence on earth.' For that we've come bearing gifts for the newborn king."

Patisar was the first of the three to step forward and worship Jesus. He was tall with a beard and wore mosaic clothing like the rest of them. He brought gold as an offering to Jesus. The second was Casper, who resembled Patisar but was much shorter. His offering was myrrh from the mountains of Ethiopia. The third was Melchior, who was strong as his beard was long. He presented Jesus with frankincense.

"These are beautiful gifts. Thank you, all," Mary said, holding Jesus.

"He has your eyes, Mary," Nathaniel said, looking at her and Jesus. "I, too, have a gift for the newborn king," Nathaniel said, breaking off three petals from the poppy corn flowers that sat on a table in the *kataluma*. Next he touched his chest, and when he pulled his hand away, a small, blue ball of light came with it.

"What is that?" I asked.

"A gift," Nathaniel whispered. "I will always be with you, Enreal, and will give my life for you if need be."

Holding the petals in one hand and the blue light in the other, Nathaniel gently began swirling his hands around each other but never letting them touch. The blue light, along with the petals, began to levitate. Nathaniel kept it close to his body. When he extended his hands out, motioning on either side of one another, he began shaping what looked a like bird, then a brilliant red light appeared. He cupped his hands together, and the light slowly faded. Upon opening his hands, there stood a young great owl.

"He's beautiful," Mary said, taking the owl gently from Nathaniel. "What's his name?"

"He is a *she*, and her name is Tigist," Nathaniel said.

"That's a beautiful name," I said as Tigist hopped over to Jesus and snuggled up next to him and fell asleep.

"What does her name mean, Nathaniel?" I asked.

"Patience—her one desire will always be to serve the Messiah. She'll always be there for him, never judging and never neglecting. She'll see to his understanding of God. Her life is forever linked to his. What happens to him will happen to her. She's a piece of me I can leave with him. Her knowledge of God is the same as my own. She is my gift to you, Jesus," Nathaniel said, looking at Tigist. "I must leave now," Nathaniel added before kissing me on the forehead and walking to the door.

"Nathaniel," I said, stopping him. "I've never thanked you for all you've done," I said kindly, looking at Jesus and back at Nathaniel.

"And you'll never have to, Joseph," Nathaniel responded, putting his hand on my shoulder before walking outside into the darkness and flying off.

The Story of Everin

Jensen

It was early morning when we returned to the States. As soon as we walked off the jet, we were surrounded by the media asking all kinds of different questions, wanting to know what happened in Saudi Arabia that would cause us to cancel the rest of the Embrace the Fate tour.

"Damn, it's good to be home," Connor said as we walked into the terminal.

"Octavia, if I could have you and the band follow me, we'll get you guys to your limo," an oddly tall man said, escorting us away from the crowd.

"That would be great," Octavia responded, "thank you."

"Boy, I sure do enjoy those laps of luxury, but I'm super happy to be home," Bear said smiling, remembering nothing of what happened in Saudi Arabia. "Well, I guess I'll talk to you guys soon," Bear said, walking in another direction.

"You're not taking the limo with us?" Dean asked, surprised.

"No. Maybe next time. I just want to go directly home. I'm super jet-lagged," Bear said as he yawned.

"All right, man," Dean said as he and Bear bumped fists.

"I wonder what the Nexus did to make everyone forget about what happened?" Dean asked, nudging me. "It almost seems like everyone who looked upon the Nexus not only forgot about what happened but became extremely tired afterwards."

"It must be some side effect the Nexus caused with the mind wipe," I answered frustrated.

"You don't look so good, Jensen," Maya said as we sat down

in the limo.

"I have so many questions," I responded, rubbing my head. "I have all these powers, and what good are they? I can't even save the people I love," I said, taking a deep breath and shaking my head in disappointment.

"I miss him too, Jensen," Maya said, fighting off her tears. "It's not your fault."

"He was my real father all along, and he betrayed us with his lies," I said disappointed.

"Sometimes lies are all we have," Maya said, taking a deep breath.

"What can you tell me about my mother?" I asked.

"I'd love to hear about Everin," Octavia said and smiled.

"So you want me to tell you the story of Everin," Maya said and smirked. "Everin is wise as she is beautiful. As you know, Everin is God's first child," Maya said recalling. "She is brave as she is loved. She has soft, white skin, jet-black hair . . . ," Maya explained, pausing. "She's perfect in every way. Where do you think you got those beautiful blue eyes?" Maya said, looking at me shrugging and smirking. "She was revered by all and became known in heaven as God's most divine angel. It's no wonder your father was drawn to her. She had such supremacy," Maya said, becoming almost jealous.

"What was Nathaniel like back then?" Dean asked.

"Nathaniel was revered by all in heaven as the wisest of all angels," Maya said. "When he spoke, everyone listened. Everyone would take his words as gospel and never question him," Maya said thinking. "I remember when he told God, Eden, and Everin that the abyss was a mistake and it shouldn't be created, that was the first and last time they didn't listen to his wisdom," Maya said, taking a deep breath. "He said that we deserved the evil that plagued heaven because we ignored the signs. Who knows how many elders were involved in the plot to remove God. When God vanished, we realized human souls were no longer coming to heaven when they died. They instead stayed as they lay. We never found out why. But I believe Jesus knew something was going to happen in heaven and that one day his descendants may need an army. Only a descendant of Christ can raise the dead."

"They say people who are cremated lose their gift of a soul,"

Connor said. "Is that true?"

"No. A cremated soul will stay where their ashes were laid in the earth, and when Christ comes again, they will be resurrected."

"What was it like to descend to earth?" Octavia asked.

"Painful. I'll never forget it," Maya answered.

Maya

I took flight. I fought hard through the jinn in my path. They came at me like a river flowing out of control. Stopping midair, I looked one last time at our once-beautiful home. When tears fell down my face, I saw a dark-cloaked figure. It set its sight on me. I became scared. I flew so fast I felt myself break the sound barrier and heard a sonic boom. Breaking through the surface of heaven, I looked back to see that the dark-cloaked figure stopped before entering the crack in the surface. I was sure I died. The first thing I remember was a bright white light and sputtering noises coming at me from all different directions. Before long I was being hit over and over by lightning. I heard thunder. Each bolt of lightning that struck hit me more intensely than the last. I prayed for the pain to stop as it was more than I could bear, but it never came. At first orange and red bolts of lightning began hitting my beautiful white wings, causing the feathers to catch fire and fall like dead leaves from a tree. Next I saw the skin of my wings melt off like water dripping off a pipe. Then I felt great pain as the bones of my wings began snapping. The pain was excruciating and terrible; I was living a nightmare. Suddenly the bones were ripped from my back and replaced with two lacerations that would become scars and serve as a reminder of something that I once was. My body began turning, and I could see the bottom of heaven. It was black, and I saw what I could only describe as little pinpricks on a black cloth with light shining through. When I hit something that felt like metal, I bounced off it and hit the pavement. Opening my eyes only for a moment, I saw a blond-haired girl in her midtwenties running over to me.

"Oh my god! Are you okay?" she shouted before shouting out to someone to call 911. "You're gonna be okay. Help is coming," she said before I lost consciousness.

***

"Any information on her yet?" a man dressed as a doctor asked a nurse standing over me and taking my vitals.

"No, Doctor," the nurse responded.

"Amazing," the doctor said.

"What's that, Doctor?" the nurse asked.

"She has to be one of the most beautiful women I've ever seen," the doctor said, looking at me.

"She is indeed very beautiful," the nurse said.

"Where do you come from?" the doctor said to himself before walking out of the room.

"Where am I?" I asked, opening my eyes.

"It's okay, ma'am. My name is Rebecca Redding. I'm your nurse. You're in the Laguna Beach Hospital," she said softly and reassuringly. "Can you tell me your name?"

"What?" I said, looking around confused. "How did I get here?"

"An ambulance brought you in," Nurse Redding said.

"Where are my clothes?" I asked as I looked down and saw that all I was wearing was a hospital gown.

"Can you tell me how you got such severe lacerations on your back?"

"Lacerations?" I asked, sitting up.

"Yes. The lacerations are on your scapulae," Nurse Redding explained.

"I have to go," I said, shaking my head scared.

"You're in no condition to leave," Nurse Redding said as I stood up and lost my balance and she caught me.

"You don't understand, I can't be here," I said, becoming upset.

"Why?" Nurse Redding asked.

"Everybody is in danger," I said panicking. "They're after me."

"Who's after you?"

"You have to let me go," I shouted. "Now!"

"You can't leave," Nurse Redding said. "The police are on their way, they need to ask you some questions."

"About what?" I shouted as she laid me down.

I began crying, remembering everything that had happened and the cloaked figure that came after me like an evil wraith.

"I'm not sure," Nurse Redding said. "I'll get you some water. I'll be right back."

When Nurse Redding left the room, I slowly got out of bed and gently stepped onto the cold floor. Taking a moment to find my balance, I walked over to a closet in the room. I opened it and saw an orange sweatshirt and a light-blue long-sleeve overall with the name "Austin" embroidered on it. Putting it on, I noticed the sleeves were too long, so I rolled them up before tucking my hair under a red Chevrolet hat and making my way out of the room. Keeping my head down, I saw a mop and bucket sitting off to the side. I grabbed it to help maintain my balance and made my way through the hospital impersonating a janitor. Seeing some security guards coming, I quickly hid in a room that had the door open. When I saw them pass, I looked behind me and saw a dark-skinned nude woman with short, black hair lying on a table. As I looked at her, I could see that this woman was someone who highly believed in God and his angels and loved her family more than anything. Putting my hand on her forehead, I saw glimpses of her life, and it was beautiful.

Suddenly I heard sniffling and someone crying outside the door. It was a young boy standing outside the room. He was around eighteen with short, brown hair and football-player-type build. I could see he was thinking hard about coming into the room. As I watched the tears roll down his face, I could see this boy was the woman's son.

"Hello," I said, walking out the door of the room.

"Hi," he said sadly, wiping his tears.

"I know what you're thinking about doing, and you don't have to go in there," I said, looking at him. "If you do, that will be what haunts you for the rest of your life," I said.

"Sometimes the things we choose not to do are the things that haunt us forever," the boy said and sniffled.

"Your mom would want you to remember all the wonderfulness she gave you and your brothers. From the wonderful beautiful Christmases, Easters, birthday parties, Super Bowl parties, you name it, kiddo. This is what she would want you to remember, how much she loved you, her husband, and your brothers," I said and smiled as he gave me a hug.

"I miss her so much," the boy said crying as I hugged him.

"Thank you for your kind words," the boy said politely, looking up at me.

"You're welcome, Preston," I said, putting my hands back on the mop and bucket and walking away.

"May God bless you," Preston said before asking. "How do you know my name?"

Turning around for just a moment, I smiled at Preston and nodded.

He smiled and whispered, "Thank you," to me.

I whispered back, "You're welcome."

Walking out the automatic sliding doors, I saw two maintenance men fixing one of them that had been completely knocked off the track.

"How did this happen?" one of the maintenance men asked the other.

"Some kid. He was super upset about his mother passing away. When they told him, he became distraught, and he stormed out of the hospital and punched the slider off the track," one of them said.

"Poor kid. I hope he's all right."

"I'm sure he is. His father came after him and calmly brought him back into the hospital."

Walking right past them, I knew they were talking about Preston. When I got to the parking lot, I watched as the shadows lifted, and there in front of me stood many jinn ready to kill me no matter the cost. Flicking my wrist, I watched as they all backed off. Standing proud, I turned and looked behind me to see it wasn't me they were afraid of.

"I saw what you did for Preston. He'll go on to accomplish wonders because of what you did for him," the being said in a female voice from behind me as all the jinn disappeared into the shadows.

"Enreal," I said, turning around and looking.

"Come with me now. I will take you somewhere safe," the being said, neither confirming or disconfirming her identity as her face was hidden behind the hood of the cloak she was wearing.

"You smell familiar," I said as I held on to her, and we took off like a bullet into the sky.

"How are you able to fly without wings?" I asked.

"You will know much about me one day. For now, just know that I love you dearly and what I'm about to do is out of love."

We soon arrived at our destination. It was a beautiful single-story home with a three-car garage and a beautiful pine tree in front of an entry gate. Walking into a courtyard past the entry gate, I saw a beautiful jasmine bush connected to a terrace hanging over a sliding glass door that looked like a small office.

"What is this?" I asked, walking up to a fountain that had a seal squirting water out its mouth.

"Your new home," the being responded, opening the front door to the house.

Before walking away from the fountain, I took a little water on my finger and touched the seal's nose, making it wet. Walking into the front door, I saw a hallway to my left. Walking down it, I looked and saw three bedrooms.

"Why are you doing this?" I asked before I heard the garage door open.

"Because I have to," the being said before disappearing.

Opening the door at the end of the hallway, which was a laundry room, I saw a truck pull into the garage. Blessed were my eyes—it was Nathaniel.

***

"Did you ever find out who or what that was that brought you to the house?" I asked.

"No," I responded.

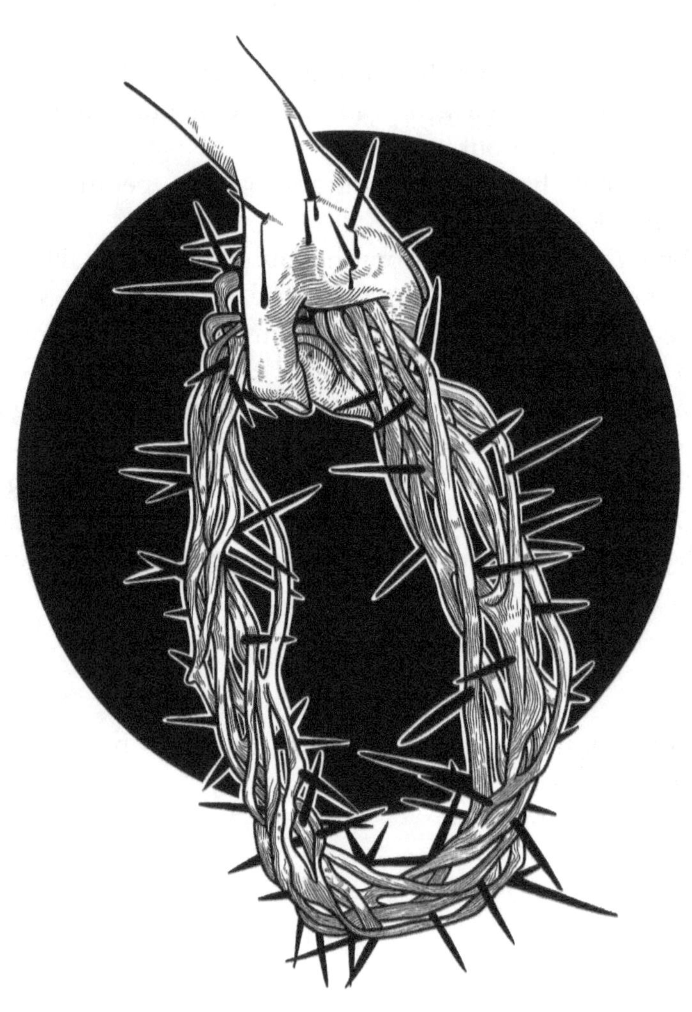

Crown of Thorns

Octavia

Three months after the unfortunate events that took place in Saudi Arabia, Embrace the Fate's self-titled album went triple platinum, earning three Grammy nominations. I remember Nathaniel once said he could see our debut album succeeding. Not long after the nominations, my mother, owner of Nuclear Bullet Records, insisted that I make a solo album. Jensen wrote all the music and supplied backup vocals as needed throughout the album, and just like that, he and I took on an all-new genre, pop. My mother called the album the best work I'd done and said I brought a certain spunk to the genre that hadn't been seen before.

Within the next two months after working tirelessly in the studio, my album came out, and I found myself being nominated for six Grammys for the solo album. While working on Embrace the Fate's new album, I thought, *What could be better than this?* We had so much money pouring in from Embrace the Fate's first album, and now my solo album, *Bleeding Rose.* I felt the need of wanting to do more. Jensen and I already had been taught at an early age to save money, and Nathaniel taught us to invest in property, as this was a side business of his that was very lucrative. I thought of how awesome it would be to set something in motion that other celebrities could stand behind and support. Bills, mortgages, college funds for people's children. I thought of how good it would feel to just come along and help someone out of their financial burdens. We could very comfortably afford $3 million a year that could help people in need. When I shared the idea with my family one night over a family dinner, it was met with some negativity.

***

"So what do you guys think of my idea?" I asked after I'd finished explaining.

"With all due respect, Octavia, I think it's really nice what you want to do, but you're talking about giving money away," Connor said, shaking his head. "Now you're asking us to do the same."

"How would we go about finding out information on these people so we could ensure we're not being taken advantage of?" Dean asked.

"Well, we'd definitely need to have a business plan written up," Jensen said.

"Well, Octavia, I think it's a very noble idea," Bear said, "especially since the economy isn't looking so good right now. We can probably help."

"And that's what I'm getting at. We could help so many people if we wanted to. This is something I think many celebrities could get behind and support. Last year Vin Diesel made $54.5 million, and Jensen and I made $23.5 million. These are both ridiculous sums of money. Jensen and I just take $3.5 million off our $23.5, we're still left with $20 million. That is still a ridiculous amount of money for one family."

"Last time I checked, Octavia, just like Vin Diesel, we earned that money, and we worked hard for it," Connor said frustrated.

"I don't know. But I would never put the words 'hard work' in the same sentence with what we do," Dean said, shrugging. "Did any of us really work that hard?"

"Construction workers work hard, slaving in the sun for eight hours a day, sometimes more, and they don't make a fraction of what we do," Jensen said, looking at Connor.

"Connor, after you fell into all this money, what was the first thing you did?" I asked.

"Does it matter?" Connor asked, rolling his eyes.

"Just answer the question," I said.

"I bought Neverland Ranch," Connor said.

"You bought Neverland Ranch?" I said, shaking my head.

"How about you, Dean, what did you buy?" I asked, looking at Dean.

"Here I am sitting and supporting you on this conquest, and I get roped into the hot seat," Dean said, taking a deep breath. "I bought Bran Castle."

"Vlad Țepeș Castle in Wallachia?" Jensen asked excitedly.

"Yeah," Dean said, looking at Jensen.

"That's awesome. When did you buy that?" Jensen asked, giving Dean a high five.

"Guys, please!" I said frustrated.

"You're right. Sorry," Jensen said. "Continue."

"So Bran Castle and Neverland Ranch. Do either one of you live in these extravagant places?"

"I do, sometimes," Dean said, getting excited and smiling.

"The fact that you're over at our house 90 percent of the time, Dean, tells me you really don't live in Bran Castle as you claim to," I said, smiling. "Nice try."

"That's why I said *sometimes*, and you don't have to worry, I won't be staying with you guys much longer. I purchased the house at the end of your street that just went for sale," Dean said and smiled. "So we'll be neighbors."

"And you, Connor?" I asked.

"I'm turning Neverland Ranch into a museum, like Graceland," Connor said, still frustrated.

"So it was an investment?" I asked.

"Yeah," Connor said, becoming short.

"How about you, Bear? How many more cars do you think you'll need before you're satisfied?" I asked, looking at Bear.

"Octavia, some of us want a little more than just a beautiful oceanfront home in the Niguel Shores."

"Let's not forget, direct beach access," Jensen said and smiled, adding to Bear's comment.

"You can say that again!" Dean said, giving Jensen another high five.

"You two are ridiculous," Bear said laughing.

"What did we do?" Dean and Jensen said simultaneously.

"You guys really are . . . ," I said, stopping midsentence and putting my hand on my forehead before fainting.

***

Waking up in a hospital, I felt that I had a bandage around my head and I was in a hospital gown, lying on an uncomfortable bed. The room was cold and dull. There was nothing on the walls except a nurse's info on a whiteboard and a television. There was a small cabinet to hang clothes in. Looking to my right, I saw Jensen sprawled out on an uncomfortable chair that turned into a bed. My arms and hands were weak as I looked down. I saw two IVs taped to my left arm. I pulled an oxygen line out of my nose, and an alarm began to sound.

"Why am I here?" I said drowsily, looking at Jensen.

"Octavia," Jensen said, quickly sitting up.

"What happened?" I asked, feeling the bandage around my head.

"Nurse!" Jensen shouted into the hall after opening the door in the room. "How are you feeling, baby?"

"What happened?" I asked again.

"You collapsed and hit your head on the dining room table. You have a bump on the back of your head."

"How long have I been here?" I asked.

"A week," a nurse said, walking into the room.

"A week!" I was shocked. "Is my baby okay?" I asked, touching my stomach.

"She's just fine, Octavia. I'm Susan. I'll be your nurse."

"Oh, thank God," I said, taking a deep breath in relief.

"You scared me," Jensen said as I rubbed my head. "How are you feeling?"

"Weird."

"Weird, why?"

"I'm trying to make sense of this dream I had."

"Was it a good dream?"

"No," I said, shaking my head. "I was sitting on sharp rocks and dusty sand. I was bleeding, exhausted, and sad. I could see that I was living out Jesus's last hours. I was wearing what appeared to be a white robe that was stained with my blood, sweat, and tears, some of it old and some of it new. I could feel pain all over my body, especially on my back. Two Sanhedrin guards were in front of me, laughing and twisting the vines of a plant together that had very sharp barbs all over it."

"The euphorbia milii," Jensen said.

"What's that?" I asked.

"It's the plant the Sanhedrin used to form the crown of thrones. The vines have extremely sharp barbs," Jensen explained.

"The Sanhedrin walked over to me, set the crown down on my head, and pressed it down, saying, 'Here's your crown, King of Jews.' They pressed down so hard it tore through the flesh all around my head, and I began to bleed severely."

'What do you think, King of Jews? Are you ready to be delivered to your final resting place?' they mocked.

'You will see me seated on the right side of my father. Then you will know, I am the Son of Man,' I said in Jesus' voice as they both spit in my face.

"They escorted me to the cross I was to carry to my final resting place. When I hauled the cross through the city streets, I had sweat mixed with blood running down into my eyes. I fell to my knees, and a sweet lady ran over and padded the sweat and blood from my eyes, until she was pulled away by the crowd. Suddenly an owl came and landed on the cross. It spoke to me and told me, 'Have strength, don't give up. We'll be gone from this place soon. But have no fear, Jesus, for they will know soon enough that you are the Lord.'

"I could see that I'd reached Golgotha. Taking the cross from me, the Sanhedrin dropped it in the sand. Pushing me to the ground, they laid me down on the cross and drove three long nails into my body. Of the three, one went into each of my wrists and the other into my feet. I'd never been so tired or weak in my life. I couldn't even scream in pain. I was so exhausted. As they stood the cross upright, I could feel the life leaving my body. I saw Judge Samantha Rouge walk up to me with a spear. She stabbed me just below the ribs on the right side of my body. When this happened, I watched from the clouds as I was already dead. I saw an angel whose face was blurred come down from heaven. I watched the angel take the essence of the nails, flying up to the clouds to give them to me. I watched as before my eyes they transformed into blades.

"It told me, 'These are called the blades of Trivium. Combine them with the Nexus, and see to the destruction of the temple veil.' I flicked my wrist, and the Nexus appeared. Holding the Trivium blades to the Nexus, I watched as they became one. I flew down from the clouds in spirit to see to the destruction of the temple veil. Once in front of the veil, I swung the Nexus and cut it down in the middle. Then came great thunder and lightning, and it began to rain. Flying back into the clouds, the angel told me, 'I don't do well having competition.' The angel quickly turned around with a katana in its hand and attacked me, but I was no match. It soon took the Nexus from me. When it slid its hand up the blade of the Nexus, it removed one of the three Trivium blades. I lunged at the angel, and it stabbed the Trivium blade into my right wrist. Taking the Nexus, it stabbed me in the left wrist. Feeling weak, I watched as the angel removed the other two Trivium blades, and the Nexus disappeared.

"'For this is the way to kill a god,' the angel said, hovering in the sky before I lost consciousness and everything became dark.

"When everything came into focus, I was kneeling beside Jesus's body, washing it and preparing it to be wrapped in a shroud and placed in a tomb. When I went to remove his crown, three of the barbs sank into my skin."

"You've been touched by Jesus, Octavia," Jensen said and smiled.

"Why me?" I asked.

"I don't know, but maybe soon you'll find out why."

"Do you think I was too hard on the guys with my idea of wanting to help people?" I asked, changing the subject.

"About that," Jensen said.

"What?" I asked.

"Well, you know how Connor wasn't digging your idea?" Jensen said.

"Yeah."

"I would say he's the biggest supporter of your idea. He's already put it into effect."

"How so?" I asked.

The Kane Foundation

Connor

Arriving at the grocery store, I grabbed what I needed and waited patiently in line when I heard a man ask the cashier if there was any way the store could help him out by giving him a discount on the baby formula and diapers he had or if they could just give it to him as a onetime courtesy.

"Please, ma'am, I'm begging you. All I need are the diapers and the formula. I swear I can come in on my next payday, which is this Friday, literally two days from now, and pay what I owe you," the man pleaded.

"Let me ask my manager," the cashier said.

"Is there anything we can do to help this gentleman out? He's a little short on cash," the cashier asked the manager.

"No, it all needs to be paid for now," the manager said rudely.

"Please, I thought I had enough money. Is there anything you can do?" the man asked again politely.

"Like I said, sir, everything has to be paid for. If you cannot pay for them, I need you to step out of line."

"What does he owe?" I asked, stepping forward.

"Hey, Connor," the cute blond cashier said, "how are you?"

"I'm good," I said, pulling out my metal Oakley money clip. "How have you been, Natalie?"

"I'm—" Natalie responded before getting cut off.

"Listen, young man, try getting laid on your own time," an old woman behind me said.

"Rude much?" I said, turning and looking at her.

"How dare you?" the old lady said grumpily.

"Natalie, just run my card to pay for his stuff."

"That's really nice of you, Connor," Natalie said.

"Well, I'm a pretty nice guy," I said as Natalie looked at me and smiled.

"Why are you helping me?" the man asked.

"Because I want to," I replied.

"God bless you, sir," the man said, shaking my hand gratefully. "The world needs more people like you."

"It's my pleasure, sir," I said before he walked out of the store, and Natalie rang up the old lady's groceries next after I let her go in front of me in line.

"So . . . back to that nice-guy stuff. Where are you taking me to dinner tonight?" Natalie asked as the old woman snatched her groceries out of Natalie's hand.

"Little slut," the old lady muttered.

"Wow, you're a crusty old buzzard, aren't you?" I said, getting mouthy.

"Listen, young man—" she said before I cut her off.

"No, you listen!" I shouted. "We've all been listening to your nasty, rude attitude. Then you call my friend a slut. Also, I, along with everyone in line, heard your trite remarks about the gentleman who couldn't afford the stuff for his baby. What is your problem? Why are you such an angry person?" I asked.

"You wouldn't understand," the old lady muttered, looking away.

"Maybe I would. Maybe I can help you," I said, following her out of line.

"Well, isn't that sweet. My problem tends to be a bit larger than just helping me out with some groceries."

"Don't judge a book by its cover," I said, looking at her. "You see the tattoos, the piercings, and you think, 'This boy is out of his mind.' I assure you, it's exactly the opposite."

"Okay. My husband and I put twenty thousand dollars down on a custom home to buy, with the agreement that we would sell our other home before our move-in date," the old lady explained.

"And that hasn't happened yet," I said.

"No, and our move-in date is coming up," she said.

"When?" I asked.

"Friday next week."

"A week and a half away."

"Yeah. If we don't sell it, we'll lose our new home and our twenty-thousand-dollar deposit."

"Can you give me the address to the house you're selling?" I asked.

"Why?"

"I may know someone interested in buying it."

"That would be great, young man, thank you," she said, writing her first and last name and the address on a Post-it note.

"Beautiful name, Mildred," I said. Then I introduced myself. "My name is Connor Kryst," I said, shaking her hand.

"My god, you're the boy who plays the guitar in the band my grandson listens to," Mildred said, becoming excited after hearing my name.

"Embrace the Fate," I said.

"That's it! That's the one! Embrace the Fate!"

"Well, Mildred, it's been a pleasure." I shook her hand and smiled.

"It has," Mildred said, pleasantly surprised. "And you, young lady, I apologize for my rudeness."

"Apology accepted," Natalie said and smiled as Mildred walked out of the store. "Listen, Connor, I see you in here all the time. You always come to check out in my line no matter how long it is," Natalie said smiling. "I've decided to make it easy on you and make the first move. So what time are you picking me up tonight?"

"Eight," I said and smiled.

"I'll be ready," she said as I grabbed my groceries and took a sticky note she put her number and address on. "See you tonight."

"See you then," I said, walking out of the store.

Walking out of the store, I was in such a good mood and looking forward to seeing Natalie. As I walked to my truck, I saw the man I'd helped earlier getting into an old, beat-up VW bug.

"Sorry to keep bothering you," I said, putting my groceries in my truck and then walking up to him. "I didn't catch your name," I asked.

"It's Thomas," the man said and smiled, shaking my hand again.

"Listen, Thomas, I'm not sure how to say this, but I think I can help you."

"With what?" Thomas asked.

"Is there somewhere we can go, maybe have a cup of coffee, and I can explain?" I asked.

"Sure. How about the coffee shop across the street?" Thomas suggested.

"Yes, I know the store manager there. Her name is Anna, she's very sweet," I responded.

"I can meet you there in about thirty minutes. I just need to take these groceries home first."

"Thirty minutes, I'll meet you there," Thomas said, confirming.

Connor

It was 2:50 p.m. I was ten minutes early to meet Thomas. I felt wonderful for what I was about to do but also scared.

"Hey, Connor, how are you?" a beautiful woman in her mid-twenties asked as I sat down at a table.

"Anna, I've been great," I said. "How have you been?"

"No complaints. Just dealing with the coffee lovers of the world," Anna said smiling. "So what will it be, or should I get you your usual?" Anna asked.

"The usual," I responded.

"Connor, do you realize that you're the only reason why I order so much peppermint into my store?" Anna said and laughed.

"What can I say? I'm a minty kinda guy," I said as Thomas walked in the door.

"Will that be all?" Anna asked and smiled.

"Yes, thank you," I answered. "Thomas, how are you?" I asked, greeting him as he walked in.

"I'm good," he said, looking at me curiously. "So what do you want to talk about?"

"I want to ask you some questions, some may be personal. But if you answer them and you answer them honestly, I promise it will be worth your time."

"Okay," Thomas said.

"What do you do for a living?" I asked.

"I do maintenance work at a luxury apartment building," Thomas answered.

"How much do you make a year?"

"Around forty thousand."

"Do you own your home?"

"No," Thomas answered embarrassed.

"How many cars do you have? Do you finance them?" I asked.

"We have two cars, one we own and the other we finance."

"Do you find yourselves struggling financially?"

"How the hell is any of this your business?" Thomas said, becoming frustrated.

"Thomas—" I said before being cut off.

"I'll bet you have no idea what it's like. Working from nine to five for a worthless check they take so much out of to cover your taxes and health insurance. You work blood, sweat, and tears, thinking maybe you'll get the next promotion that would see you and your family out of the financial burdens of life. But no! That promotion goes to the guy you just trained. That doesn't have half the experience you do."

"I'm sorry if I upset you, Thomas," I said, apologizing to him. "I have only one last question."

"What?" he asked, taking a deep breath, tiring of the questions.

"How much do you owe on the car you're financing?"

"Around eighteen thousand," Thomas said. "Why?"

"Because I'm going to write you a check to pay it off."

"I'm sorry, what?" Thomas asked surprised.

"I'm writing you a check. I think twenty thousand should cover it," I said.

"Is this some kind of joke? Why would you do that?"

"Because I can," I said. "And I do know what it's like to work in corporate America. Now take out your phone and text me your address and you and your wife's full names."

"Why would I do that?" Thomas asked, scared, not sure where this was going.

"Because after I see what you do with the check, I need to know who I'm gifting the house I just bought to," I said as Thomas texted me the information.

"Is this one of those insane candid camera things?" Thomas jokingly laughed. "Are you gonna ask me to kill someone for you?" Thomas asked, smiling but serious.

"This is nothing like that," I said, standing up handing him the check. "Cash the check. Pay off the car. I will be in contact with you soon."

Shaking hands with Thomas, I went to go pay the bill when I began talking to Anna.

"So that's it for today?" Anna asked.

"That'll do it," I said and smiled at Anna.

"How come you never ask me out, Connor Kryst?" Anna asked flirtatiously.

"What can I say, I'm a shy guy," I said, flirting back.

"Well, we've put it out on the table now," Anna said.

"And?" I asked smirking.

"And . . . what do you mean, 'and'?" Anna asked.

"I was totally ambivalent just now," I said and laughed.

"You're a weird guy, Connor."

"And I was totally kidding. What time are you off on Saturday?" I asked.

"Nine," Anna answered.

"What do you say I pick you up at nine Saturday and take you to a movie?"

"That would be lovely."

"I'll see you Saturday then," I said, giving Anna a hug before walking out.

***

Two dates and four weeks later, I found myself head over heels in love with Anna. I loved spending all my free time with her. I also bought the house from Mildred so she and her husband could move into the custom-built home they'd invested in. When I'd seen Thomas had cashed the check, I did some investigating to see if he'd paid off the car or just pocketed the cash. After discovering that he paid off the car, I put things in motion for the house I bought from Mildred to be gifted to Thomas and his wife, Simone.

Thomas

Simone and I were at such ease because of the generosity we were shown by Connor Kryst. Sitting down in the backyard with a box of Einstein bagels, Simone and I laughed and enjoyed each other's company. We also talked about making a trip to Germany where we both had family, now that we could possibly afford it without a car payment over our heads.

"I wonder when you're going to hear something from Connor again?" Simone asked while feeding their five-month-old daughter, Eva.

"I'm not sure," I said as the doorbell rang.

Answering the door, I was greeted by a man in a suit and tie who looked like a lawyer. He was tall, very handsome, and well-groomed.

"Is this the residence of one Thomas and Simone Grossman?" he asked.

"I'm Thomas," I said politely.

"Thomas, I'm Pierce Hatchet. I represent the Kane family," he said. "May I come in?"

"The Kane family?" I asked, confused.

"Connor Kryst," Pierce said, looking at me.

"Oh my gosh, you're a friend of Connor!" I said excitedly.

"May I come in?" Pierce asked again.

"Yes, sure, where are my manners? Come in please," I said, inviting Pierce inside. "Honey, this is Pierce Hatchet."

"Ma'am," Pierce said and politely shook Simone's hand.

Walking into the kitchen, he set his briefcase on the dining table and opened it, pulling out a small stack of papers.

"Okay," Pierce said, setting the papers down. "My client, Connor Kryst, was very moved that you did what you were supposed to do and paid off your car with the money he gave you. He has decided to extend his generosity," Pierce said as he flipped through a couple of the pages. "This is the deed to your new home Connor purchased with the intent of gifting it to you."

"Oh my god, honey!" Simone said excitedly, beginning to cry. "Where did you find such an angel that would do this?"

"I can't believe it," Thomas said shocked.

"Believe it. All I need is a couple of signatures, and the home is yours."

"So . . . I have to ask, where is all this generosity coming from?"

"Not long ago, Octavia Kane, Connor's sister, shared an idea of helping people in need. Since then, the Kane family has made it their business to do just that."

"Thank you so much," Simone said when she walked over and held Pierce's face in her hands before hugging him.

"I assure you, ma'am, I will pass your gratitude on to the Kane family," Pierce said politely. "Now here's my card. If you have any questions, please don't hesitate to give me a call."

The Grammys

Octavia

When we received our invitations to the Grammy awards, I was eight and a half months pregnant, and I felt like a whale. I was mentally done with this pregnancy.

"Octavia, are you ready to go? The limo will be here any second," Mom asked as I walked downstairs to see Maya fixing Dean's tie on his tuxedo.

"Wow," Jensen said, smiling at me when he looked at me coming downstairs, "you look absolutely beautiful."

"Really, or are you just saying that because you're my husband?" I said pouting. "I don't want to go."

"Sweetheart, you look beautiful," Mom said smiling.

"Mom, is Dad going to be there?" I asked.

"No, sweetheart," my mom responded.

"He should be, this is only one of the most important days of our lives," I said angrily.

"Sorry, baby," my mom said as Jensen gently caressed my back.

"I'll be waiting outside," I said, walking out the front door, away from everybody.

"Why is she so mad?" Connor asked, fixing his tie. "It's just Dad. We all know the way he is."

"She's pregnant," Mom said, shaking her head.

"I suppose we all have you to thank for this," Dean said, patting Jensen on the back smiling.

"Me? I didn't do anything," Jensen said as we all walked out the door.

"Well, that bun in the oven didn't just get there on its own," Dean said as Jensen looked at him awkwardly before walking outside and getting in the limo.

When we arrived at the Grammys, there were fans and photographers everywhere. When the driver opened the door, Jensen stepped out first and then extended his hand out to help me. When I stepped out of the limo, the crowd went wild, cheering aloud.

"We love you, Octavia!" a young girl shouted.

Walking onto the red carpet, Jensen and I turned for photographers to take our picture.

"Sorry about that," Jensen said after backing up into somebody.

"No worries," the man said as Jensen turned around. "Jensen and Octavia Kane," the man said smiling. "Embrace the Fate, right?"

"Sully Erna," Jensen said, looking at the man.

"In the flesh," Sully said as he smiled, looking at us both. "We should get a picture together," he said, nodding before grabbing Octavia and me both and turning to the photographers.

"Holy . . . ," Dean said star-struck as soon as he saw Sully. "Oh my god, Mr. Erna, I'm such a huge fan," Dean said, walking up to shake his hand.

"The feelings are mutual, Dean," Sully said, shaking Dean's hand. "Pleasure to meet you," he said politely before beginning to put his attention elsewhere.

"Sully Erna just said it's a pleasure to meet me," Dean said, looking at Bear and Connor. "Did you hear me?" Dean said, getting Bear's attention.

"Ah, hell, are we gonna be dealing with this all night from you?" Connor said, looking at Dean and Bear laughing. "This guy, so easily . . . star-struck," Connor said as he lost his train of thought as Rihanna walked past him.

"And you say I'm bad," Dean said, putting his arm around Connor and walking further down the red carpet.

Making our way down the red carpet to the double doors that entered the seating area of the Grammy awards, we were greeted by an employee wearing a tuxedo.

"Octavia Kane," he said, pausing for a moment, looking at his clipboard. "I'm going to need you to come with me. You're going to be presenting an award with Adam Levine," the employee said, talking to me.

"All right," I said, kissing Jensen before following another employee backstage.

"This way, sir," another employee said, showing Jensen and the guys to their seats.

When I walked backstage, there were celebrities everywhere I looked. I felt as if I should have been impressed, but I wasn't as I felt I was one of them now.

"All right, Octavia, if you can wait here," the employee said, walking away.

"You're Octavia Kane, right?" a slender and tall beautiful woman asked, walking up to me.

"Céline Dion?" I gasped and smiled.

"How do you do?" she asked, shaking my hand greeting me.

"I'm good," I said. "How are you?" I asked nervously.

"I'm wonderful. How many months are you?" Céline asked, gently touching my stomach.

"Eight and a half months," I said, touching my stomach. "I'm finally getting down to the end."

"Children are such a blessing, Octavia," Céline said and smiled before walking away.

"Octavia," a man said, walking up to me.

"Adam," I said as he put out his arm for me to interlock mine with his. "We're on, right after Adele is done with the opening performance."

"Are we still on for next week to record the new song I told you about?" Adam whispered politely in my ear.

"Absolutely," I said as I kissed him on the cheek.

"You're the best, Octavia. Are you nervous?" Adam asked, looking at me and putting his hand on mine.

"Yeah, I've never done this before," I answered.

"You'll be fine. Just read directly off the teleprompter," Adam said as Adele closed her performance. "You'll be fine. I'll be with you the whole time."

"You got this, Octavia," Céline said smiling as she walked by again.

"Adam, Octavia, are you ready?" an employee standing next

to Céline asked. "Three, two, one, you're on," he whispered.

As Adam and I walked up to the curtain on the stage, I grasped his arm tight.

"Careful not to cut my circulation off." He smiled and looked at me out the corner of his eye. "Everything is going to be fine, Octavia," he whispered.

"Now, presenting the award for Best Music Video, Adam Levine and Octavia Kane," Hugh Jackman announced.

When the curtain opened, everyone cheered as Hugh Jackman walked up to us, stopping only a moment to give me a gentle kiss on the cheek. I looked at the crowd and saw Jensen and the rest of my family sitting in their seats fifth row from the front. When Jensen and I locked eyes, it was as if we were the only two in the auditorium, and all my fears went away as he gave me a little smile.

"The nominees for Best Music Video are," I spoke into the microphone.

"Eminem for," Adam said into the microphone, "'Renegade.'"

"Beastie Boys for," I said, "'Where I'm From.'"

"Lady Gaga for," Adam said, "'Satan's Kiss.'"

"And Kid Rock for," I said, "'Tennessee Love Song.'"

"And the award goes to . . . ," Adam said and paused.

"Eminem for," I said and smiled at the crowd, "'Renegade.'"

As the audience applauded, Eminem stood up and made his way to the stage, shaking hands with people on his way up as everyone stood to give him a standing ovation.

"Thank you," Eminem said as he kissed me on the cheek and accepted the award from Adam.

When we walked offstage, we were escorted back to our seats, and as I sat down, I felt nauseous.

"You looked great up there," Connor whispered as Jensen smiled and kissed me.

"Thank you," I replied.

About an hour into the Grammys, an employee came over to our seats and asked if I could accompany him backstage. Walking backstage, I was met by the host, Hugh Jackman, and the Grammy director, Louis Horvitz.

"Hello, Octavia, how are you?" Louis asked politely.

"I'm good," I said, wondering what they wanted.

"Adam Levine had to leave quite unexpectedly, and Maroon 5 was scheduled to perform tonight. Any chance you'd be interested in filling the slot?" Hugh said. "He highly recommended you."

"Um," I said, nervously biting my lip.

"She'll do it," a voice blurted out.

"Sir, you can't be back here!" an employee said sternly.

"You got this, babe," Jensen said, walking up to us. "This is everything you've worked for, to perform at the Grammys. Do you know how big of an accomplishment that is?"

"Okay," I said smiling. "I'll do it, under one condition," I said to Louis and Hugh.

"And what's that, young lady?" Louis asked.

"Embrace the Fate performs," I said as Louis took a moment to think.

"What are you doing?" Jensen said, looking at me shocked. "This is your time, not ours."

"I won't do this without my family," I said, looking at Jensen, Hugh, and Louis.

"Okay," Louis said. "Sounds intriguing."

"I'm sure we're in for quite a treat," Hugh smiled.

After getting the guys together, we explained what was going on and took the time to tune the instruments that were supplied to us.

"Octavia, are you sure you want to do this?" Connor asked.

"I'm sure. We all started this together," I said, looking at all of them as they all came around and hugged me together.

"So modest. She's already walked away with 60 percent of all the awards tonight," Dean said and laughed.

When the curtain opened, Jensen immediately opened with playing the synthesizer, softly finding the pace and tune and slowly getting stronger as one by one they all started playing their instruments while I looked out at the crowd.

***

(Octavia sings, metal sound.)
'Twas the night before
A battle for the world
No words, just demons crying
I rode the wildfire
'Twas a blazing pyre
Now that our worlds collide
You think you found the answer
For I'm the necromancer
Forget the poetry
The cancers in the world
Now we're living in desperate times

(Octavia sings chorus, metal sound.)
I've got a voice that will never fade
I've got the dreams and innocence of every
man
You'll see me soaring across the blue, blue sky
You'll dream of me beneath the moonlit sky
I've got a story that you need to read
I am the memory that you hold deep

(Octavia sings, metal sound.)
Returning from that journey
An unknown destination
I'm the tale they've read to you
When it starts the night
I'll battle the jinn and hellfire
I'll banish them to the depths of hell
A man's imagination
It's a dream emporium
Just think of all the tales they've read you
It's the story you can't escape
While you intoxicate
The cold thought of just living in desperate
times

(Octavia sings chorus, metal sound.)
I've got a voice that will never fade
I am the dreams and innocence of every man
You'll see me soaring across the blue, blue sky
You'll dream of me beneath the moonlit sky
I've become the story that you need to read
I've become every memory that you hold deep

(Octavia sings operatic, instrumental.)
Forever
The voice
That will never fade
Innocence
Of this world
Dream of me
Innocence
Of this world . . .

(Octavia sings, metal sound.)
I've got a voice that will never fade
With the dreams and innocence of every man
You see me soar through blue, blue sky
Breaking through your moonlit sky
I am the story that you need to read
I am the memory that you hold deep . . .

(Voice fades out slowly.)

***

"Thank you!" I shouted to the crowd as the lights dimmed and our performance ended.

"That was fantastic, Octavia!" Louis said excitedly. "You have a rare voice indeed."

When the curtain closed, we were escorted back to our seats. When we sat down, Jennifer Lopez was sitting behind us. Slowly leaning forward, she whispered, "Great job Octavia, that was a wonderful performance."

When the Grammys were coming to a close, we saw Céline

Dion and Dr. Dre take to the stage.

"The last awardee of the night will be crowned Best New Artist . . . ," Céline Dion said. "And the nominees are . . ."

"Stereo Head," Dr. Dre announced.

"Octavia Kane," Céline said and smiled.

"The Mark Thompson Band," Dr. Dre said.

"Embrace the Fate," Céline said as Dean jumped out of his seat and cheered.

"Reggie K," Dr. Dre said.

"And the award goes to . . . ," Céline said with an enormous smile. "Embrace the Fate."

As our music began playing throughout the auditorium, everyone jumped out of their seats to give us a standing ovation. Making our way to the stage, we stopped to shake many hands and hug other celebrities along the way.

"Wow, words can't express how happy we are to be up here right now. Our fans, I'd like to shine the light on you tonight. Because without you, none of this would be possible. Nuclear Bullet Recorders, Mom, I love you," I said as tears began to fill my eyes. "And to my husband, who's up here right now to help accept this award, you are my best friend, and I love you more than words could ever define."

Suddenly, midsentence, the rap artist Lord Lucious got out of his seat in the second row and began slurring his words and shouting profanities at everyone, especially us. Stumbling onto the stage, he ripped the microphone out of my hand and continued his rant.

"Don't worry, Octavia, I'm gonna let you finish. But let's be real, Reggie K was the greatest new artist of the year," he shouted when suddenly a fist made contact with his face and he was knocked out cold.

"Go ahead, sweetheart, finish," Jensen said, straightening up his jacket and tie as everyone in the crowd applauded him for silencing Lord Lucious.

"Thank you, everyone, and good night," I said as Jensen kissed me and, like a gentleman, took my hand and escorted me offstage.

While stagehands helped walk Lord Lucious offstage, a security guard came over to where we were sitting.

"Mr. Kane, I'm going to have to ask you to come with me," the security guard said as everyone in the audience began booing at the security when Jensen stood up and was put in handcuffs.

As Jensen stood up, I noticed he was standing in a puddle of water.

"Oh my, where did that come from?" the security guard asked, looking down.

"Oh my gosh, my water broke," I said as Dean and Connor both helped me stand up.

"The baby is on its way," Jensen said excitedly, smiling. "Is there any way you can uncuff me? If you do, I promise to come down to the police department and turn myself in," Jensen said as Louis walked up to us.

"Uncuff him, son," Louis said to the security officer. "Quick, get out of here before I change my mind," Louis said and smiled after the cuffs were off.

"Thank you," Jensen said, shaking Louis's hand.

Enreal Is Born

Jensen

The lightning struck, and thunder roared. It came from out of nowhere. It was like nothing I'd ever seen. The rain and wind were so strong that not only were trees dancing but cars and buildings shook. As the wind passed between the narrow passages of the buildings, it made the most terrifying noise as it sounded like a titan waking from its slumber. I stood looking out the window of the hospital room. I was shaken up, nervous but excited. I wondered, *Who would our daughter look like, Octavia or I? Or would she be the perfect mix of us both?* What lingered in the back of my mind was, *Will the jinn know of her birth? Is she a threat to them, or will they just continue to come for me?* These were the unanswered questions that haunted me.

"Jensen, go be with Octavia," Dean said, walking up behind me, taking off his jacket and rolling up the sleeves of his tuxedo. "I'll keep watch."

"Do you think they'll come for her?" I asked Dean for his opinion.

"Not if they know what's good for them," Dean said, taking a deep breath.

"You're right."

"Of course, I'm right," Dean mocked. "Why would you ever question it?" he laughed.

"Where is everyone?" I asked, looking around.

"They're in the waiting room."

"Mr. Kane, we're ready if you'd like to come in now," a nurse said, handing me scrubs to wear.

"I'm gonna look like a smurf," I said, taking the scrubs and laughing.

"Shut up, you'll look great!" Dean said as I put it on. "Never mind, you do look like a smurf," Dean smiled. "Now go get in there," Dean said before giving me a hug.

"Before I go, I've been meaning to give something to you. I think your mom would've wanted you to have it."

"What's that?" Dean asked as I flicked my wrist and the spear of destiny appeared.

"This belonged to your mother. It rightfully belongs to you," I said as Dean took it and the cross with Jesus looking out from it appeared on his left bicep.

"Dang! That hurts," Dean said as he looked at the tattoo. "Now get in there and welcome your daughter into the world," Dean said as we hugged, and I went into the room.

When I entered the room, I gently kissed Octavia and lightly caressed her cheek. She had her legs up in stirrups, and Dr. Childs walked in.

"All right, Octavia. I think we're about ready," Dr. Childs said, checking Octavia's dilation. "Okay, Octavia, go ahead and push."

As Octavia pushed, the thunder outside became loader, and the rain came down more violently than before.

"What is it?" Octavia asked as I looked around suspiciously.

"I'm not sure," I said as Octavia then screamed in pain as she continued to push.

"Something isn't right," Dr. Childs said.

"Doctor, something's wrong," a nurse said, concerned but also confused.

"What?" Dr. Childs asked.

"I don't hear a heartbeat," the nurse said.

"What?" I screamed, terrified.

"That's impossible, the baby had a heartbeat just a moment ago," Dr. Childs said.

"Are you saying—" Octavia said before being cut off.

"We have to get the baby out, right now!" Dr. Childs shouted at the nurse with urgency.

***

Dean

As I stood looking out the window, I saw the shadows, trees, and streetlights begin to shake. I could see it was unnatural, something elusive.

"I knew you'd come," I said, still looking out the window after feeling the presence of someone.

"Did you?" a voice said from behind me.

"Lancaster," I turned around and smiled. "When did you get here?" I asked, shaking his hand and giving him a hug.

"Yesterday," Lancaster said.

"And you're just now gracing us with your presence," I said, shaking my head, still smiling.

"I had some other things that needed my attention," Lancaster responded.

"It's good to see you," I said as I walked past Lancaster.

"Where are you going?" Lancaster asked.

"There are things outside that need my attention," I said.

"Need help?" Lancaster asked.

"If any of them need communion, I'll be sure to let you know," I said jokingly.

"Funny," Lancaster said. "Be careful."

"Careful," I repeated, "Careful is my middle name."

"Careful isn't even in your vocabulary," Lancaster said.

When I walked outside, I flicked my wrist when my spear appeared. The lance Jensen gave me appeared at the end. It was a beautiful rustic gold. When the shadows all around me turned to jinn and reaper warriors appeared, I looked at one of the demented freakish creatures they had with them. It was a black lion. It had two heads and devilish-looking claws that looked more like sharp talons. When it moved, I could see it had wings with sharp barbs all over them.

"Dean Rouge," a reaper with a big scar across its face said in a deep voice, stepping forward.

"And you are?" I asked ready to fight. "Ah, wait. I remember you. Saudi Arabia, right?" I said, sarcastically smiling. "I can tell by that big, nasty scar on your face," I paused before continuing, "you know, if you don't stop picking it, it'll never heal."

"Enough talk, traitor. We come with a message," the creature said firmly.

"Do I look like an answering machine?" I said, cracking a joke. "Ah, rough corral," I said, taking a deep breath jokingly.

Without warning, the reaper began attacking me, trying to hit me left and right with a bloodied cleaver. When the black two-headed lion jumped on me and began trying to rip me to shreds, I flicked my wrist, and my spear disappeared. I was able to get the upper hand. I held my fist to its chest and flicked my wrist. When my spear appeared again, it went directly through the chest of the two-headed lion, and it fell to the ground dead. With the reaper still trying to hit me, a female godlike entity walked up, and the reaper just stopped its attack.

"It's a good thing you came, or else I would have—" I was saying till the godlike entity suddenly grabbed me by the neck and lifted me into the air.

The more I fought, the more its grip tightened, till it held its hand to my chest. A brilliant green light appeared, and I saw flashes of myself fighting a young girl with a dutch french braid on a rooftop, and my spear had become a lightning bolt that I was wielding as a weapon.

"Our work is done here," the godlike entity said, dropping me on the ground.

Flicking its wrist, it nodded, and all the jinn and reapers disappeared into the shadows.

"That's not much of a message to deliver," I said, mouthing off.

"You are the message, Dean," the godlike entity said, turning around, kicking me in the stomach, sending me flying through the air till I landed on the street.

"I'm still standing!" I shouted, coughing up blood and standing back up when I was hit by a car.

Jensen

When the baby came out, she looked as if she was in a deep sleep. She looked calm and peaceful but did not move even when the doctor poked and pinched her to see if she could get a response. As I took her into my arms and brought her over to Octavia, we couldn't help but cry.

Together we kissed our daughter several times, praying she'd just wake up from her deep sleep, but she didn't. When the doctor took her from us, she laid her down on a table on the other side of the room. She and the nurses began a sequence of different procedures to get a response from her.

"I can't believe this is happening!" Octavia said, frustratedly crying. "Please, God, please don't let this happen."

As I comforted Octavia and felt the loss of our daughter, the lights in the building began flickering and then shut down completely before suddenly just coming back on. The walls began shaking as the earth shifted from side to side. It lasted about a minute until all the shaking stopped. Then we heard the sweet sound of our daughter's cry.

"Oh my god," Octavia began crying aloud.

"My sweet baby girl," I said smiling as tears came down my cheeks, and I took her from the doctor.

"She's perfect," I said, looking at Octavia, "just like her mother."

"We did it, babe," Octavia said, smiling before taking a deep breath.

"No, you did it," I said, smiling and giving her a kiss before Octavia took another deep breath. "Are you okay?"

"This took a lot out of me," Octavia said, suddenly breathing heavily and shaking her head. "Something's wrong, Jensen," she said after it became increasingly hard for her to breathe.

"What is it?" I asked frantically.

"I can't breathe," she said, shaking and panicking. "I can't breathe," she said over and over, gasping for air, and her whole body began shaking.

"Nurse!" I shouted, running into the hallway panicked.

"Jensen, what's wrong?" Alyssa shouted terrified.

Putting my arm out to brace her from falling off the bed, I held her as if I were hugging her with our daughter coddled in the other. Suddenly a nurse ran into the room and quickly began giving Octavia oxygen.

"Sir, I need you to move, I need to get to her arms," the nurse demanded.

"Doctor, we need you here now!" one of the nurses shouted over the phone in the room.

"What is going on here?" Dr. Childs asked shocked, walking into the room as we all just stood there shocked.

"She's going into epileptic shock!" Dr. Childs shouted.

"What do you need?" the nurse asked.

"Restrain her from falling, she has to go through it," Dr. Childs said.

"Are you serious? That's the best you can do?" Alyssa shouted. "That's my daughter!" she shouted, crying as Connor hugged her.

"Miss, you must trust my judgment and remain calm," Dr. Childs said. "It will pass. I promise you."

Suddenly it passed just as Dr. Childs said it would, but Octavia didn't wake up.

"What's wrong with her? Why isn't she awake?" Connor asked.

"I've never seen anything like this," Dr. Childs said, getting on the phone in the room.

"I'm going to need everyone to leave the room," one of the nurses said firmly.

"What?" Alyssa shouted upset, shaking her head. "Absolutely not! I'm staying right here with my daughter."

"I understand," the nurse replied. "But only you, okay?"

"Sir, can I have the baby? I need to take her to run some tests," she said calmly, taking my daughter from my arms. "Would you like to accompany me? I'm taking her to the nursery."

After about twenty minutes, Alyssa came out from the room with the doctor. When I saw the look on her face, I knew something was wrong.

"So, Dr. Childs, what's going on?" Connor asked as soon as he saw the doctor.

"Octavia has fallen into a coma," Dr. Childs said, shaking her head, "due to the pressure that was put on her brain during the seizure."

Alyssa suddenly began hyperventilating, and Maya went to comfort her.

"I'm so sorry. We are going to do everything we can to figure this out."

"What are the chances she'll come out of it?" I asked, trying to be strong.

"A coma can be tricky, and there's no telling when or if she'll wake up," Dr. Childs said.

"The best thing for her is that you all remain positive and calm."

"Are you telling me that I may never see my wife again?" I asked, crying and rubbing the back of my head.

"It's a possibility, sir," Dr. Childs answered.

"Jensen, are you okay?" Dean asked, being strong when he saw I was emotional.

"I don't think I can take this," I said, leaning up against a wall and dropping my head into my hands.

"Did you see baby's blue eyes yet?" Dean asked, putting his arm around me.

"What?" I asked, shaking my head, upset and confused.

"Just wait till you see her, Jensen. I saw those beautiful blue eyes of hers, and that was all she wrote. She's absolutely breathtaking."

"I was already with her in the nursery," I said, taking a deep breath as tears rolled down my cheeks.

"Thank God, she looks like her mother, right?" Dean said happily, trying to lighten the mood.

"What happened to you?" I asked, looking at Dean, seeing he looked beaten and hurt.

"Jensen's got a point, Dean. Where have you been, you look like a train wreck?" Connor added.

"I got hit by a car, but who cares about that. Let's go see the baby," Dean said and smiled. "Lancaster is at the nursery now."

"When did he get here?"

"Not long ago," Dean said. "Maybe he can say a prayer for Octavia."

"That'd be nice," I said and smiled.

After a couple of hours, I walked to the cafeteria to get a cup of coffee and something to eat.

When I was done and was walking back, I saw a nurse enter Octavia's room.

"Hello," I said as I walked in and saw the nurse about to deliver something into Octavia's IV. "What is that you're giving her?" I asked curiously and stretched. "Maybe you didn't hear me. I asked, what are you giving her?" I asked again firmly.

When the nurse looked at me, her eyes were glazed over black. Wasting no time, I flicked my wrist when suddenly she held a knife to Octavia's throat.

"Wow, what the . . . ," Dean said shocked, walking into the room.

"She will never fulfill her destiny. With one jerk of my wrist, I could end it all," she hissed.

"Then why haven't you?" I asked, scared but wondering.

"Quick, take the knife from me, I don't know how long I can hold it back," the nurse said, twitching, handing me the knife. "There is another that has gone for your daughter," she added before falling to the floor.

Running out of the room to the nursery, I saw everything was calm until a woman dressed in dark red jumped out from the glass window of the nursery holding my daughter. She held a katana unfamiliar to me. Flicking my wrist, I engaged her until I saw that she wasn't the enemy. She was protecting my daughter, and there was another possessed nurse inside the nursery Lancaster was struggling with. Flicking my wrist again, my crucifix appeared, and the possessed nurse began shouting blasphemies.

"Keep that away," it said in a raspy voice as I tossed the cross to Lancaster and I grabbed the possessed nurse.

"You've seen this cross before, haven't you, reaper?" Lancaster said firmly, walking up to it. "Release her!" Lancaster said, pressing the cross to her forehead and holding it there.

Before my eyes, I watched as the jinn expelled itself from the young nurse by shooting out through her eyes. As I gently cradled her to the floor, I looked up at the woman holding my daughter.

"Thank you," I said, looking at the woman. "Wait a second, you're that reporter that talked to Octavia in Saudi Arabia," I said, taking my daughter from her.

"What happened here?" a security guard asked, abruptly running up to us.

"I'm not sure, sir. This nurse just suddenly collapsed," I said shrugging.

"And the window, how did that get broken?"

"I'm not sure," I said politely. "If you don't mind, I need to talk to my friend here," I said as Lancaster intervened with the security officer before I grabbed the woman by the arm and marched her into another room.

"Who the hell are you?" I demanded.

"My name is Athena Goodwater," she said as she looked at my daughter. "I'm Godric's sister. What is her name?" Athena asked, continuing to look at my daughter.

"What are you doing here?" I asked and ignored her question.

"I'm here to help your daughter," Athena answered, looking at my daughter. "But I don't have long. What's your daughter's name?" Athena asked.

"Danika," I said.

"Danika Kane is the key to everything," Athena said, looking at Danika. "May I hold her?"

I was hesitant, but I allowed it, thinking if she were going to harm her, she would have done it by now. Handing Danika to Athena, she cradled her.

"I am very happy to meet you, young lady," Athena said, looking at Danika. "Do you have the elder grimoire in your possession?" Athena asked, looking up at me.

"Always," I said.

"I would like to insert an entry, if you don't mind. Then I must leave, I don't have much time."

"What entry?" I asked, flicking my wrist, and the grimoire appeared.

"The origin of the Goodwater family and how Godric came to discover the Nexus and cement a legacy for his family. I will tell of the beginning as it was told to me and tell of the Nexus as I remember it."

The Nexus

Athena

Long before the Great War in heaven, two beings of great power and strength named Rowlis and Zamael created two weapons in the shape of revolvers to battle four giant monsters that threatened their planet and citizens with slavery and madness. The monsters became known by the citizens as the Titans. The Titans were ruthless and cunning and knew nothing of love and forgiveness. They identified themselves as Rhea, Lysander, Ares, and they answered to Zeus. Zeus, being the vilest among them, proclaimed himself to be the ultimate power, and no other Titan dared challenge him. When Rowlis and Zamael stood against them, Zamael, standing valiantly, mortally wounded Zeus when she shot him in the chest with her revolver. Zeus, in one last desperate attempt to kill Zamael, threw a thunderbolt; but when she dodged it, it pierced the planet's core, and before the Titans met their end, Zeus prophesied his return and vowed to rid the world of Rowlis and Zamael.

Knowing their planet's core was unstable and dying from being hit by the thunderbolt, Rowlis and Zamael set out among the stars to find a new home suitable to their people's needs. Searching endlessly, they finally found a planet and quickly began ushering citizens there. But some refused to leave the dying planet and eventually met their fates when the planet turned into a black hole.

Rowlis and Zamael named their new home Arthonia. It was a beautiful place of waterfalls, springs, and flowers as far as the eye could see. Arthonia was also home to a very beautiful stone that would glow purple at night, and sage commonly grew around the stones. At times the sage would fuse itself to the stones. Rowlis and Zamael looked at the stones as a thing of beauty and purity, naming them Sage Stones. The stones became very sacred among the citizens. But there were those who believed the stones were more than just sacred objects. They believed the mystic stones were magical and held answers to lifelong questions about the universe, and they became known as Majestics. The Majestics believed that at one point in time, Arthonia might have been home to an almighty master of the universe and that the stones, although beautiful, were magical weapons.

For decades there was peace and tranquility in Arthonia—until, in the blink of an eye, Arthonia was met by an unimaginable evil. Four entities identifying themselves as Apocalyptic Horsemen raised their weapons up and warned Arthonia that they were the keepers of time and that they came with the intent of bringing about the demise of Arthonia. Standing in their path of violence were Rowlis and Zamael and one family of Majestics known as the Goodwaters. Together they met the entities with an iron fist. While Rowlis and Zamael fought the Horsemen with the revolvers, the Goodwater family used ordinary weapons against the Horsemen until, by chance, Oric Goodwater discovered the Horsemen's weakness to the Sage Stones. Oric imprisoned the Horsemen to four different Sage Stones, but not without casualty. During the battle, Rowlis had been stabbed in the chest by one of the Horsemen who called himself Death. For days Rowlis suffered in agonizing pain because the blade was coated in a poisonous toxin known as Marafol.

After having a revelation of a descendant of the Goodwater family, Rowlis shared his divulging revelation with Zamael, and they together called upon Oric and Talia Goodwater.

"It won't be long now," Zamael said, trying not to cry, holding Rowlis's hand.

"Zamael, I'm so sorry," Talia said saddened.

"These so-called Horsemen were stronger than any foe Rowlis and I have ever faced, and we fear for the security of Arthonia and the universe."

"We beat them though," Oric stated, trying to convince her of our victory.

"Did we?" Zamael asked. "I fear that all we did was trap them," Zamael said, wiping her tears. "Rowlis believes that the fate of the Horsemen's demise rests within a Goodwater descendant not yet born of this world. He has made a decision to best help your descendant. He must merge his life force with his revolver."

"Why have you called upon us?" Oric asked.

"Because I've decided to do the same," Zamael said, looking down.

"Why would you do this?" Talia asked frustrated. "Why are you giving up?"

"We're not giving up, Talia," Zamael said, taking her hands. "It's imperative that your descendant is successful. The fate of this universe rests within this person."

"Who will watch over Arthonia?" Talia asked confused.

"Arthonia will be left to you, the greatest of the Majestics, the Goodwaters," Zamael said and smiled.

"We can't be responsible for this," Oric said, shaking his head. "I don't agree with what you're doing."

"You don't have to agree," Zamael shrugged. "You will do what I ask."

"I'm unsure of how to rule," Oric said scared.

"Oric, it's okay to be scared," Rowlis said, touching Talia's stomach. "Treat Arthonia as you would your children—you nurture, you guide, you forgive and love." Rowlis smiled before taking a deep breath and closing his eyes.

We looked on and watched as Rowlis disappeared and all that remained was his revolver.

Saying goodbye one last time, we hugged Zamael and told her we loved her before she, too, merged with her revolver. Moving into Rowlis and Zamael's beautiful kingdom and taking over their responsibilities wasn't easy for us or the citizens. Citizens were resistant at first and untrusting, but when we ruled justly and held strong to Rowlis and Zamael's ways, we won their respect and trust. Locking the revolvers away, we swore to keep them safe until the day the descendant would come and claim them.

Godric

I was born to a big family, and with that came many obstacles. But none of those obstacles were as hard as being the middle child and having an older brother and a younger sister. I constantly struggled to find my place in the world. I was so much more eccentric and venturesome than my brother and sister. And I constantly found myself at odds with my father.

When I turned eighteen, it was by chance that while adventuring in the unknown mountains of Arthonia with my sister Athena, I fell into a hole in the earth. It was as if Arthonia had swallowed me. When I hit stairs and tumbled down them, I thought, *What would stairs be doing in the ground on a mountain?* The stairs were something from long ago as they were aged and weathered. The only light in the cave was that of where I'd fallen in. Looking at the walls, I saw symbols carved all over them as if they told a story.

"Godric, are you okay?" a voice asked, coming from where I'd fallen in.

"Athena, come down here," I said as she jumped down.

"What is this?" she asked, looking at the walls, standing beside me.

"I don't know, but it's fascinating. Just look at the details," I said, staring at the symbols. "It looks like writing."

"What is that?" Athena said, pointing nervously at a sword with a slight curve to it.

It sat atop an ivory pillar. It was so beautiful.

"Don't touch it," Athena said, scared as I came really close to it.

Looking closer at the ivory pillar, I saw more writing and symbols.

"Do you hear that?" I asked, gazing at the sword and gently running my fingers over the writing on the pillar as they began to glow.

"What?" Athena asked, looking around and then back at me.

"There's something here," I said, continuing to touch the pillar.

"You probably shouldn't do that," Athena said scared.

"What?" I asked.

"Don't touch that sword," Athena warned.

"It speaks to me," I answered as I picked it up and it began to glow bright green.

"Yeah, maybe you should put it down," Athena said nervously.

As I went to put it back down on the pillar, it became hot, and I couldn't let it go. The ivory pillar sank into the floor, and the walls began to shake as if the cave was beginning to collapse. I was trying everything to let go of the sword. It suddenly began to melt, creating an ooze-like substance that flowed all over my body till it found its way to my bloodstream by seeping into my pores. Then a burning pain came in waves, hitting me and causing me to drop to the floor. My body tensed up.

"Godric!" Athena screamed. "I'll get help!" she shouted, running back to the opening and climbing out.

Lying there and breathing softly, I saw a vision of a young girl holding this same sword. I could see she was strong as she was beautiful. When the pain slowly went away, a warm, tingly feeling came over me. I stood up and cracked my neck, and I felt very different. I looked down at my body, and it appeared to be more masculine than normal. Thinking that I needed to catch up to Athena, I suddenly shot into the sky like a rocket. Without any control, I flew all over the place. After focusing, I got more control over myself. Hovering in the sky, I saw Athena running back to the marketplace that surrounded the kingdom. Flying to her, I dropped down right in front of her.

"Oh my god," Athena said shocked.

"I should've listened to you and not touched the katana," I said, putting my hand out, motioning her to stop running.

"What's a katana?" Athena asked confused.

"It's what the sword calls itself," I answered.

"It talks to you?" Athena asked.

"Yeah. It means no harm," I answered. "It also showed me a vision of a young beautiful girl. Her name is Danika Kane. The katana said it belongs to her."

"What happened to you?" Athena asked, looking at my appearance.

"I don't know. But I'm able to fly."

"Obviously," Athena said, "and your physique has definitely

improved."

"Yeah."

"We must tell Father," Athena said, turning to walk away.

"No, Athena, we mustn't!" I said sternly, grabbing her arm.

"Let go of my arm, Godric," Athena said.

"I'm trying," I said, panicking.

"You're hurting me," Athena said as she also began to panic. "Let go!" she shouted and pushed me so hard I fell to the ground. "What just happened?"

"You pushed me," I said, getting up off the ground, brushing myself off.

"I feel different. What was that blue light that shone in between your hand and my arm?"

"Oh no," I said worriedly.

"What do you mean, 'oh no'?" Athena asked.

"I think . . ."

"Think what?" Athena asked as I scrunched my teeth together. "Oh man, you mean I got this same crap you've got?" Athena asked. "Do I look different?" Athena said scared.

"No," I said, thinking. "Think about flying," I said, getting an idea.

"Why? Why would I think about flying?" Athena asked as she shot off into the sky.

Flying after her, I told her to focus and remain calm and everything would be okay.

"You just had to touch me, didn't you?" Athena asked frustratedly.

"I'm sorry," I said awkwardly.

"I wonder what else we can do," Athena said, becoming intrigued.

"I don't know, but why don't we find out?" I said, flying off into the clouds.

Enjoying our new powers, we tested ourselves to endless limits. We discovered that I merely just rubbed some of my powers off on her, and there was no telling how powerful I was as flying was all Athena inherited.

"Your powers may be beyond Rowlis and Zamael," Athena said, hovering in the sky.

"They may also be beyond the Titans and the Horsemen," I

said, thinking.

"Do you think one of the Horsemen could have been a second coming of Zeus?"

"I can tell you this, Zeus, Rhea, and Lysander betrayed their father Kronos and gained some kind of immortality. But whether one of the Horsemen was Zeus, I don't know. The katana belonged to Kronos it's called the Nexus and whoever wields it becomes a master of the universe."

"So the Horsemen were here for the Nexus?"

"I believe they were. Before Kronos's children betrayed him and absorbed his power, he set the Nexus atop an ivory pillar and placed a spell on it."

"How were you able to get past the spell?"

"The pillar read but four names on it: 'Godric, Nathaniel, Jensen, and Danika Kane.'"

"Besides you, who are those other people?"

"I don't know. But I love the name Nathaniel. One day, if I ever have a son, I will name him that."

"What are we going to tell Father?" Athena asked.

"I'll have to avoid him until I figure something out. You don't look any different, so you should be fine," I said, confused and scared.

After avoiding my parents for weeks, I saw a vision of the destruction of Arthonia. It was then that everything inside me told me to get the revolvers. I went to the chamber where my father kept the revolvers of Rowlis and Zamael, and once there, I took them. As I grabbed each revolver one at a time, I watched as they both disappeared as the Nexus had. Over the course of the weeks, I came to call the katana the Nexus and learned that when I flick my wrist, the Nexus would appear, and when I'd think about the revolvers and flick my wrists, they would appear.

***

Not long after, my father called on us. I knew it was about the revolvers. Frightened, I found a dark-blue cloak to hide my appearance and walked into the throne room of my father's kingdom.

"My children, the revolvers of Rowlis and Zamael have

gone missing. You three besides your mother and I are the only ones that have access to the room they rest within. One of you is responsible for this travesty," Oric said firmly before his eyes faintly glowed a light red. "One of you has taken them, and I'm going to find out who."

"Father, your eyes," Koric said before suddenly Oric snapped and grabbed him by the neck.

"Oric!" my mother screamed, running up to stop him.

"Enough!" I shouted, taking the hood of my cloak off, revealing my face.

"Godric," my mother said faintly.

"You took the revolvers," Oric asked as if he already knew the answer, "and woke me?"

"I did . . . Rhea," I said, calling her out. "Now drop my brother."

"Did you just say Rhea?" my mother asked, looking at me.

"Are you challenging me, boy?" Rhea asked angrily.

"You're damn right, I am," I said firmly as Rhea dropped Koric.

"So where are the revolvers, boy?"

"They're safe."

"Don't play with me!" Rhea said, grabbing my mother.

"Release her!" I shouted, flicking my wrist.

"The Nexus?" Rhea said frightened. "Keep that away, boy!" Rhea shouted petrified.

"It looks familiar, doesn't it? The power of the Nexus runs through my veins now, and the Titans and Horsemen are finished! I'm the ultimate power here," I shouted, putting my hand on Rhea's shoulder. I flicked my wrist again, and this time a Sage Stone appeared.

"Noooo!" Rhea shouted while her whole body lit up in a bright white light, and she was once again cast to the Sage Stone. All that remained was Oric.

"Father," I said, looking at him and flicking my wrist, and the stone disappeared.

"Godric?" he asked, shocked, putting his hand on my shoulder before smiling. "What happened to you, son? How were you able to display such awesome power?" he asked, looking at me.

"We have much to discuss, Father."

***

Koric

As years passed, citizens became angered by Godric's powers. Whether out of jealousy or fear, I'm unsure. Citizens began speaking of concerns that if Godric ever wanted domination over Arthonia, he could take it. I knew his days of being among us were becoming limited as I could see him with heavy thoughts of leaving us.

"Why are you sad, Godric?" I asked.

"I never asked for these powers," Godric said. "I don't like being hated by the citizens."

"I don't hate you, brother," I said.

"I've made up my mind, I'm leaving Arthonia," Godric said sadly.

"Where will you go?" Koric asked. "Will you search the galaxies of space, possibly move from planet to planet as Rowlis and Zamael did?"

"No, I will create a new place, residing over the entire universe," Godric said. "I will call this place, heaven."

"And who would rule over this heaven, brother?" I asked.

"I'd be its creator," Godric said, deep in thought.

"Have you spoken to Father about your plans?" I asked.

"I have, and neither he nor mother understands," Godric replied.

"Have you told Athena?" I asked.

"Told me what?" Athena asked, walking up behind us.

"Godric has decided to leave us, sister," I said.

"You're allowing the citizens to get to you," Athena said frustratedly.

"There's more to it than that," Godric said.

"Really, Godric, and what is that?" Athena asked annoyed.

"As long as I stay, the citizens will remain restless," Godric said, "and the Sage Stones can't stay here. Every day they do, they grow weaker."

"So you're taking those with you to protect us?" Athena

asked.

"I am," Godric replied.

"Well, I still don't understand, and I definitely don't agree with you," Athena said mad. "If you leave, your family will be restless," Athena said. "Don't you care?"

"Athena, I must go," Godric said as Athena turned and walked away from us upset.

Godric

For days Athena ignored me. When finally the day came that I decided to leave Arthonia, everyone I loved and cared about was there to see me on my way, except Athena. I could see some citizens were upset and some relieved by my departure.

"Are you sure you want to do this, Godric?" my mother asked while she held my hands.

"I'm sure," I replied, hugging her.

"Here are the Sage Stones," my father said, handing them to me in a brown satchel.

"Thank you, Father," I said as our mother began to cry.

"I don't want to say goodbye," my mother said, looking me in the eyes.

"So let's not," I said as our father comforted my mother. "It's okay, Mom," I said concerned.

"Tell Athena . . . ," I said, thinking, "I love her."

"I will," Koric said before giving me a hug.

"Well . . . ," I said pausing, "I guess I'll be seeing you." I smiled before shooting off like a rocket into the sky.

"I didn't know he could fly," Koric said chuckling.

"I don't think any of us did," Mother said and smiled.

"Godric!" Athena shouted, hovering in the sky in front of me. "Why are you doing this?" Athena demanded.

"I knew you'd meet me up here," I smiled.

"Answer me, brother!" Athena said firmly. "I know you are not leaving because of the citizens. I demand you tell me the truth."

"The legacy I will forge lies elsewhere," I said explaining, "within a direct descendant of myself. This Danika Kane girl, I believe, is that descendent, and I must leave her a legacy of supremacy. I can't do that here."

"How did you get Father to give you the stones?" Athena asked, looking at the brown satchel.

"He listened to reason," I said calmly.

"Where will you go?"

"I'll set out among the stars," I said. "As Rowlis and Zamael once did. Keep your powers a secret, Athena," I said as I gave her a kiss on the cheek. "I leave you with one last gift."

"And what's that?" Athena asked.

"When I'm gone, flick your wrist," I smiled and shot off like a bullet into the sky.

Athena

I hovered in the sky and watched him from a distance. He looked like a star hurtling through space, and he was as bright and everlasting as the sun. When I flicked my wrist, a beautiful katana appeared. It looked similar to the Nexus but was slightly different. It called itself . . . the Arthonian.

Unforgivable Sins

Octavia

Raising my head up, I felt water mixed with mud and slug roll down my face, and I began to gag till I vomited mud and water. I continued to cough and choke until I took a deep breath, and my eyes filled with tears. The trees and bushes in this place had no leaves, just dry limbs; life was absent here. I appeared to be in the middle of a dying forest. As the moonlight beamed down through the dead trees, it cast shadows everywhere. The wind howled and echoed through the forest, and I felt cold. Looking down at myself, I saw that I was naked.

"There, there," a female voice said.

Scared, I thought, *What would someone else be doing here in this dreadful place?*

Then came the sound of terrifying shrieks and screams that carried on the wind as if someone was being brutally mauled by someone or something.

"Don't panic," the female voice assured me.

Looking through the darkness about six feet away from me, I saw a girl in her mid-twenties, wearing sunglasses and a black beanie. She was holding a black oversized coat. The brown jacket she wore was unzipped, and underneath I could see a pink T-shirt with the comic book character Harley Quinn on it. She had blue jeans and knee-high black boots. She had a bow and a quiver full of arrows. When she turned her head, I thought I saw her beanie move abruptly.

"Where am I?" I asked as she draped the oversized coat around me as if she knew she was going to find someone out here.

"Shhh, don't talk!" she said, sternly putting her hand over my mouth and looking around. "Nothing is as it seems. Your body is still in the land of the living," she whispered, taking her hand off my mouth. "Beasties can smell that, and if they catch you, they'll rip you to shreds, and you'll die in the land of the living," she said. "Then you'd just be one of the damned, like me, and would have to walk this underworld forever aimlessly without purpose."

"One of the damned?" I asked, looking at her before being cut off as this dark place suffered what felt like an earthquake.

"Shhh! Did you feel that?" the girl whispered. "Enreal is here. We need to get something straight right now," she said firmly, looking at me. "If you do exactly as I say when I say it, I can keep you alive," she said, looking around oddly.

Shortly after, we heard a scream.

"Do you hear that?" she whispered.

"Yeah," I said scared.

"Whoever screamed like that must have seen one of my sisters," she laughed sinisterly. "But you've got me," she continued, acting as if she were reassuring me of something.

"What is your name?" I asked.

"You can call me Meddy," the girl said.

"I'm Octavia," I said.

"Never gaze into her eyes, or you'll be turned to stone," Meddy said, taking a deep breath while babbling. "I'll take you to Rylin. He will know if you're the one," she said as a flying creature with snakes for hair tried to snatch us with its long, sharp talons.

"One of the three gorgons!" Meddy shouted. "We need to run."

We took off running. I was scared out of my mind as the creature flew down again, this time landing right in front of us.

"Keeping this one all to yourself, Meddy?" the creature asked with a hiss before Meddy shot an arrow at it.

Catching the arrow midair, the creature broke it with one hand.

"You know how important this one is, she could be my ticket out of this place," Meddy said.

"Not till you have killed Enreal will you be free, and as you already know, Euryale and I are arguing over who will kill her first."

"And what if it's me?" Meddy said, getting mad.

"You're not powerful enough to beat her," the creature hissed.

Suddenly, from out of nowhere, another creature with deadly black eyes and snakes for hair ran up and grabbed the other by one of its wings and threw it to the ground.

"Euryale!" the creature shouted angrily.

"Stay away from Meddy, Stheno."

"But she has—" Stheno said, before being cut off.

"She has nothing until Rylin says she has something," Euryale said angrily.

"We must run!" Meddy shouted again, looking at me as the two creatures fought and argued.

After running some distance, we came across a cave. We went in and took refuge in the shadows.

"You need to tell me what the hell is going on," I said, freaked out. "Gorgons? Am I in the twilight zone?" I asked scared.

"This is no twilight zone. You are dealing with the gorgons in this place—Stheno, Euryale, and their younger sister, Medusa."

"This is a joke, right?" I said and smiled.

"No. This is very real," Meddy said. "I have to get you to Rylin," she added as a creature came from out of the darkness.

"Cyrus," Meddy said as the creature came up to her, and she started petting it.

"What is he?" I asked looking at him.

"He's a gargoyle," she said.

"What's he doing in this place?" I asked.

"He saved Rylin's life after the fall of heaven. Now come. I will take you to Rylin," Meddy said.

"That name Rylin sounds so familiar," I said thinking.

Walking through this dark evil place with Cyrus leading the way, I looked and saw a clearing with long blades of grass. I continued to hear the wind making terrible sounds as it blew, and with it came violent screams and a hissing voice telling me to do terrible things. Suddenly I heard what sounded like an infant crying, and I could see the blades of grass shake and move as something quickly ran through it to get to the cry.

"The beasties love babies," Meddy said sinisterly. "There we are, Rylin's home," she said as I saw someone watching us from a distance.

"Who is that out there?" I asked as Meddy looked up.

"Oh, him, that's Samael," she replied. "He doesn't think much of Rylin," she said when a man came walking out from the front door of the house dressed in a black T-shirt and jeans, sipping something hot from a cup as I could see steam coming out the top of it.

"Who's that out there?" the man shouted.

"Rylin, it's me," Meddy said.

Suddenly Cyrus ran up to Rylin, whispering something in his ear. I then saw Cyrus shake his whole body as if he were shaking water off himself. Before my eyes I watched as Cyrus transformed into an even more monstrous creature. He now had horns coming out from his head, a barbed tail, wings that had barbs all over them, and his feet were long, sharp talons.

"Make sure you don't move," Meddy said, watching Cyrus come up to me and smell me.

"Have you seen Samael?" Rylin asked.

"He's been following us ever since I found this girl," Meddy said.

"Have you seen your sisters?" Rylin asked.

"They have already made an attempt to get this girl," Meddy said.

"Your sisters?" I asked confused.

"Samael has never shown that much interest before," Rylin said. "Octavia, won't you come in?"

"How do you know my name?" I asked.

"Because he felt the earthquake," another man said, walking up behind us. "You've committed unforgivable sins against your brethren, Rylin," the man said through the darkness.

When I looked up and saw the man, he was dressed in a navy-blue trench coat, wearing a cowboy hat. He had a groomed long beard and brown hair coming out from underneath the sides of the hat.

"Samael, I was wondering when you'd grace us with your presence," Rylin said, looking at him. "Which tells me, now I've finally found the right one," Rylin said before looking at me.

"You really should come inside. The beasties here aren't keen on humans, even if you are the chosen one," Rylin said, taking my hand like a gentleman.

"Rylin, you know I can't let you take her," Samael said firmly.

"And why's that?" Rylin sneered.

"I can see now why Nathaniel expelled you from his presence," Samael said and smiled.

"Don't you say that name to me," Rylin said, becoming enraged. "It's because of him I'm even in this place."

"I knew that I've heard of your name. You were the coward that left Nathaniel and the other elders to die in heaven," I said, becoming upset. "Deceiver!"

"You have committed unforgivable sins," Samael said.

"That was a long time ago," Rylin said.

"Maybe we should all just calm down," Meddy said.

Suddenly, from out of nowhere, I saw Cyrus jump on Samael, and immediately he started trying to kill him, but Samael threw him to the ground.

"I'll warn you once. Don't try that again," Samael warned Cyrus.

"Let's see how you fare against me," Rylin said as he ripped the shirt from his back and became a werewolf, jumping at Samael.

I saw him deflect all the blows that came at him. Cyrus once again jumped back into the fight, and together they tried to kill Samael.

Looking over my shoulder, I saw Meddy was nowhere to be found. Cyrus continued trying to bite at Samael's face till suddenly Samael caught his jaws. I watched as he ripped Cyrus's jaws open, and the top portion of Cyrus's head was torn from his body. Rylin continued his attacks till Samael flicked his wrist and a katana appeared, and he swiftly stabbed Rylin through the chest. When the dust settled, I saw Samael brush himself off as Rylin lay on the ground in his true form, in a puddle of his own blood.

"Rylin, don't speak," Samael said, kneeling down and holding his hand.

"Samael, I'm sorry that I wronged you," Rylin said. "Do you think you can forgive me?"

"Compassion and forgiveness," Samael said as Rylin slowly vanished, "is all I have left."

"Come, Octavia, we must get you to shelter," Samael said

standing up.

"Where are we going?" I asked. "Where's Meddy?"

"Meddy?" Samael asked.

"The girl I was with," I said upset.

"Forget what you think you know about that girl," Samael said, taking my hand and leading me in another direction.

"Where are we going?" I asked, pulling my hand away from his.

"My place," he said. "You'll be safe there."

After walking a short distance, we came upon a clearing. There in the middle of the clearing sat a little cottage that looked to be carved out of a fairy tale. With smoke coming from a chimney that smelled of pine, the house had beautiful moss spots growing on it. When Samael opened the door, it made a scary loud, creaking noise. Looking around, I saw a brewing pot hanging over a fireplace. Before closing the door, another gargoyle ran up to the house.

"Braxton," Samael said.

"What?" Braxton asked.

"Great companion you are. Where have you been?" Samael asked frustrated.

"Around," Braxton replied.

"Never around when I could've really used your help."

"Don't whine, Sam," Braxton said. "You're still alive."

"Gargoyles," Sam scoffed as Braxton walked into the house on his hind legs.

"Your place is beautiful," I said, looking around.

"Thank you," Sam said.

"What is this place?" I asked while getting warm by the fire.

"Perdition," Braxton said.

"I believe she was talking to me," Sam said, looking at Braxton.

"Was she though? Or was that a question for anyone wanting to answer it?" Braxton said, mocking Sam.

"How long have you two been together?" I asked.

"Decades!" Sam said.

"Centuries!" Braxton said.

"Forever!" Sam and Braxton said simultaneously before cracking up laughing.

"Perdition is the place where those who have committed the gravest of sins come to live out their nightmares and fears," Sam said.

"Why am I here?" I asked. "I haven't any sins."

"You will know when the one has entered perdition when you feel a quake," Sam said.

"That very quake he speaks of was felt over an hour ago," Braxton said.

The Sheath

Samael

" At a time when heaven was at its most vulnerable, God—being the only supreme being in existence—gave the elder angels godlike powers, and they in turn helped to govern heaven's realms. Rylin didn't agree with the elders being given such awesome power. He spoke out against the elders, and to speak out against the elders was to speak out against God himself. But there was one elder that Rylin loathed above all others."

"Nathaniel," Octavia said.

"The very sight of Nathaniel made Rylin's skin crawl," Sam said explaining.

"Why did he hold such anger and resentment toward Nathaniel?" I asked.

"Because he was everything Rylin wanted to be but never could. Nathaniel was the most beloved and respected angel in all of heaven—Rylin hated that. At the end, when Rylin stood with us during heaven's darkest hour, I'd never seen an angel so scared. There were jinn all around us hiding in the shadows of God's once-beautiful home. Then from out of the shadows a dark entity appeared on the balcony of God's home. It was holding a female angel by the back of her neck," I said, recalling the memories.

***

"Nathaniel, don't believe him, it's lies! Escape this place!" the female angel shouted.

"You shut your mouth," the entity said, punching her in the ribs.

"Nathaniel," Maya said worriedly, "it's Eden."

"Listen to me, Elders. Lay down your katanas and surrender, or you will meet the same fate as your friends," the entity firmly demanded.

"Nathaniel, what should we do?" I asked concerned.

"You dare threaten her life?" Nathaniel shouted angrily, grasping his katana.

"Oh, I dare," the entity said in a dark, eerie voice. "Now surrender."

"Nathaniel, you mustn't!" Eden shouted.

"This conversation is over. Kill them all!" the entity shouted.

***

"Before our eyes, I watched as this dark entity slit Eden's throat, and as she bled out, her lifeless body was dropped from the balcony. Hordes of jinn came flying toward us. As we stood tall and brave, it wasn't long till all that remained were the elders and Rylin. Scared out of his mind, Rylin abandoned us and ran. The last words Rylin heard over the wind that day were from my lips, calling him a coward. Then when I felt I was truly at my end, I made a sacrifice to help clear a path for Nathaniel to get into God's home. After I'd cleared the way for Nathaniel, he'd thought I'd fallen. And I would have, had Braxton not saved my life. He fought the jinn off me, but not before we both fell through a crack in heaven's crust and descended to earth after Maya flew down from the sky like a bullet penetrating the crust. There were flickering lights everywhere, and the pain I felt on my wings was so excruciating I lost consciousness. When I awoke, I was in perdition."

"Why?" Octavia asked.

"Because I, too, have committed the gravest of sins," I said, looking down, thinking. "I deserve to be in this place."

"What could you have possibly done?" Octavia asked.

"I was there at the beginning," I said, deep in thought, "tempting Adam and Eve in Eden's garden. I can't tell you how many times I tempted Jesus. But he is strong. He never once listened to me, and I tempted him over and over," I said looking at Braxton.

"Lucifer?" Octavia asked, looking at me.

"In the flesh," I answered.

"You don't seem like anything the Bible makes you out to be," Octavia said.

"Oh, trust me, the Bible is accurate. After Jesus was baptized by John the Baptist, I tempted Jesus for forty days and forty nights in the Judaean Desert. But Jesus refused all my offerings. I didn't agree with what God was putting him through and the strength God and Nathaniel spoke of when talking about him was superior to ours. After Jesus left the Judaean Desert, he returned to Galilee to begin his ministry. When God found out about what I had done, he showed mercy on me. He said that one day I'd be able to make it up to Jesus by helping him, but that day never came, until Jesus's return was prophesied upon the Nevillin. When I came here to perdition, I began having vivid dreams of a young girl that would one day come here in need of help."

"Samael," Octavia said.

"My given name till I fell from grace. After I committed these acts, God forbade anyone from leaving heaven again without his permission."

"How did Rylin come to be here?" Octavia asked.

"He'd fallen through the same opening in the crust as Braxton and I had, but he awoke from a coma in a hospital on earth. When he was discharged, he didn't know what to do. For years he roamed the streets, living in shelters and eating what others threw away. He did what he had to do to survive . . . until fate happened. While begging for money outside a recording studio in West Hollywood called Nuclear Bullet Records, he saw a thief snatch a young woman's purse and take off running. Running after the thief, he began to catch up to him, and out of the corner of his eye, he saw a man in a business suit running behind him, shouting at the man with the purse. It was then that Rylin jumped on the thief and took him to the ground."

I narrated the events to Octavia as they happened.

***

"What the hell, man!" the thief shouted, scared of getting up off the ground.

"That purse, it doesn't look good on you," Rylin sarcastically told the thief.

"Yeah, well, I'm pretty sure my fist will look good in place of your face, old man," the thief said as the man in the suit ran up, and Rylin fought with the thief over the purse.

Muscling the purse from the thief, the thief took off running in the other direction, and Rylin turned to the man in the suit.

"Rylin?" the man in the suit asked awkwardly.

"How have you been, Nathaniel?" Rylin asked, taking a deep breath.

"It is you," Nathaniel said. "I should kill you for what you did," Nathaniel sneered, grabbing Rylin by the neck and throwing him up against a wall.

"Spare me the lecture, Nathaniel. Next you're gonna tell me that had I stayed, things would have been different?" Rylin said, hitting Nathaniel's hands off him.

"Why, Rylin?" Nathaniel asked. "Why did you run out on us?"

"Because I was scared!" Rylin shouted, becoming upset. "Not all of us were created as tough as you, Nathaniel," Rylin said. "I did what I had to do to survive."

"I understand," Nathaniel said taking a deep breath. "Are you hungry?"

"What?" Rylin responded confused.

"You may be a coward, but even cowards have to eat," Nathaniel said.

Walking across the street to a small diner, they sat and ate lunch, and Nathaniel explained what he'd been doing with himself over the years.

"So what now?" Rylin asked when they finished eating.

"I don't know. Do you have a place to stay?" Nathaniel asked.

"I live on the streets. Every now and then, depending on the weather, I stay at a shelter," Rylin responded.

"I have a casita you can use until you figure something out. Just so you know, Maya will be opposed to helping you."

"She's still alive?" Rylin asked. "Who else made it?"

"Just Maya and I and . . ."

"And who?" Rylin asked.

"It's better if you see him for yourself."

When they arrived at Nathaniel's home and went inside, Rylin saw Maya sitting on the couch and three toddlers, all around the same age, playing on the floor with hot wheels.

"Well, well, well, if it isn't the coward," Maya said, unhappy to see Rylin. "I just have one question. Why?"

"I was scared," Rylin said, shaking his head in disappointment.

"Now here you are," Maya said, "with your hand out."

"I never asked for help," Rylin said, looking at Maya and then the kids. "Who are they?"

"That's Octavia, Connor, and Jensen," Nathaniel said, pointing them out one at a time.

"Are they yours?" Rylin asked.

"Jensen is. The other two, we're just babysitting for some friends," Nathaniel said.

"He looks like you," Rylin said, looking at Jensen and then back at Nathaniel.

"So I'm told," Nathaniel responded.

"He has Everin's eyes," Rylin curiously said. "Is he her child?"

"Yes, she died shortly after giving birth to him," Maya said.

"I'm so sorry," Rylin said.

***

"Using the casita they offered him for the night, he went to bed. Having a vivid dream of the dark lord, it told him that he was to go to perdition and wait for the time when Enreal would arrive there. When he awoke the next morning, his nightmare had come to fruition. As he was being attacked by a werewolf, it bit him, and he was left with an awesome power afterward. He was then able to shapeshift into the werewolf, and he never forgave Nathaniel as he believed it was him that put him here."

Octavia

After sitting and talking awhile, I got up and looked further around Sam's home.

"You've been busy," I said, looking at the trophies on the walls in his home of all kinds of different monsters' heads.

"What can I say, you get bored and suddenly you're hunting down witches, vampires, werewolves, any kind of supernatural entities in this place."

"So what do we do now?" I asked stretching.

"We wait," Sam said, taking a deep breath.

"So what is this person, who is *the one* supposed to do?"

"They will deliver the sheath to Enreal."

"Has there been anyone whom you thought to be *the one* before me?" I asked.

"Only two."

"And where are they?"

"Turned to stone, as they looked into the eyes of your friend Meddy," Sam said. "After she discovered the two before you weren't of importance. I believe, now that Enreal has arrived, it will mean the end of this place," Sam said as perdition rumbled from another quake.

"Meddy is Medusa?" I asked.

"Yes, and she along with her sisters believe if they kill Enreal, they will be free of this place and be set to pillage earth. Enreal has killed one of the sisters already. As she kills them off, the sheath will become more brilliant."

"The sheath?" I asked as it suddenly started to appear in my hand. "Why does this appear to me?" I asked.

"The sheath will appear to the mother of Enreal," Sam said.

"Mother?" I asked shocked.

"Yes, Octavia, you're the one. Enreal is your daughter."

"Why is she in this place?" I asked, shocked and tearing up.

"I don't know why she is here, Octavia. I just know this is the way I can help Christ," Sam said as we suddenly heard a violent scream from outside.

"I have to help her," I said, racing out the door.

"No, Octavia!" Sam shouted, running after me. "You mustn't."

Running into a grassy dark clearing, I saw Meddy taking aim at a young girl on the ground holding a knife; she no longer was wearing a beanie, and her hair was snakes hissing every which way.

"She has a Trivium blade," Sam said, looking at Braxton.

"Meddy, no!" I shouted as she looked at me with her piercing eyes.

As soon as our eyes met, my whole body became stiff as if I were covered in stone. Still having use of my arm, I threw the sheath to the young girl on the ground when she looked at me. When she caught it, immediately a katana appeared, and she ran toward Meddy. I watched as Sam ran over to me saddened.

"I'm so sorry, Octavia," Sam said as he held my hand.

"I'm just glad I got to see her at least once," I said as the lower half of my body turned to a complete stone.

As the stone slowly made its way up to my neck, I saw the young girl run over to us.

"Tigist, I need you," she said as an owl flew down from a tree and landed on the girl's forearm, and Sam walked over to where Meddy had been slain. I watched as the young girl closed her eyes and gently placed her hand on my shoulder. Slowly I felt the weight of the stone release me.

"We must leave now," Sam said, walking back to the house.

"Do I know you?" the young girl asked, looking at me.

"I don't think so, sweetheart," I said, trying not to cry as we followed Sam to the house.

Walking in the front door, Braxton startled the young girl as he was standing in the living area by the fire.

"What the . . ." the girl jumped, grabbing her katana from the sheath she now carried.

"It's okay," I said, putting my hand on her shoulder.

"What is that thing?" she asked.

"Thing? I am no thing. I am a gargoyle. Show some respect," Braxton demanded, becoming frustrated.

"I apologize," she said politely, putting her katana back in her sheath. "You just startled me."

"Startled you? I nearly jumped out of my skin," Braxton said. "Would you care to warm yourself by the fire?"

"Thank you, Braxton," I said and smiled at him, walking over to the fire with the young girl.

"Your tattoos are beautiful," I said, looking at her wrists as we sat down.

"Thank you," the girl said quietly, looking at her wrists and touching them.

"What's your name?" I asked.

"Danika," she answered, looking at me out of the corner of

her eye. "Danika Kane."

"That's a beautiful name. My husband knew a young girl once named Danika," I asked as she looked at the owl that followed her inside. "Is she yours?" I asked, noticing her look at the owl.

"Yes, she means the world to me. I just haven't been very good to her lately."

"What's her name?"

"Tigist."

"How did you and Tigist come to be in this place, Danika?"

"The thought of being alone," Danika said, beginning to cry. "Valerie was everything to me. She was my life, my love, my world, and just like that, she was taken. I tried living, but everywhere I'd look, I'd see her. When I'd slept, I'd dream of her. I couldn't go on anymore without her," Danika said, showing me her wrists and becoming emotionally distraught, "and the more evil creatures I killed, the more my rage flared at the evildoers."

"How did you come in possession of one of the Trivium blades?" Sam asked.

"I was being attacked by a horde of jinn and reapers. When they all stopped their attack all the sudden as a dark shadow fell from the sky. The dark shadow told me in a scratchy voice that I belonged at its side. Before calling off its horde it gave me the Trivium blade. I took the blade months later and cut my left wrist, and my right wrist, I cut with the Nexus," she said sobbing, taking the sheath off her back.

Taking Danika into my arms, I held her and let her cry. Looking at Sam and Braxton, I saw them both shake their heads sadly as I handed the sheath to Sam, and the Nexus disappeared.

"The Nexus will no longer appear to you without the sheath, Danika," Sam said, handing the sheath back to her.

"Where did the sheath come from?" I asked.

"Long ago, before it was a sheath, it was a cup—a grail to be exact. This grail became the most-sought-after holy relic in history. Wars were fought over it, religions fought for it. Till suddenly it vanished from existence and returned to the rightful owner."

"So what now?" I asked. "What must Danika do to leave this place?"

"In order to leave perdition and return to whence you came,

you must forever trade places with someone still in the land of the living," Braxton said, looking at me.

"Take this, you will need it. It is the Filius, it was the katana given to me by God. Combine it with the Nexus," Sam said, after flicking his wrist, and the Filius appeared.

"I'll make the trade for her to return to the land of the living," I said immediately.

"Why would you do this for me?" Danika asked confused. "I don't deserve it."

"Yes, you do," I said and smiled, holding her hands. "It just breaks my heart that I'll never see you grow up," I said, beginning to cry.

"What?" Danika asked, still confused.

"Can you do something for me?" I asked before giving her a hug.

"Anything," Danika responded.

"Tell your father," I said as Danika slowly began to vanish, "I love him."

"Why would you say that?" Danika said, looking at me with tears in her eyes. "Why did you say that?" she repeated.

"I love you, Danika," I said crying. "I love you so much, baby girl."

"Mom," Danika said shocked, looking at me before she completely vanished.

***

Jensen

As I sat there in a chair in Octavia's room, moments away from dozing off, I was startled by the sound of alarms ringing and monitors going off. Suddenly her doctor and some nurses came running into the room.

"Doctor, she's flatlining!" a nurse shouted.

I stood there and watched as they tried to bring her back. When tears began to roll down my face, I heard her say one last thing:

"I love you, Danika. I love you so much, baby girl."

It was then that I knew she was gone.

Aftermath

Dean

It's been a year since Octavia passed away. Jensen fell into despair after he suffered her loss. Shutting everyone out, he spent much of his time surfing. He once told me, "The ocean is where I feel closest to Octavia." When he wasn't surfing, he could always be found at the cemetery. In his solitude, I believe he found a sense of comfort and stability. Seeing Danika I feel hurt him further as she reminded him so much of Octavia, but in that hurt, he would often find solace.

"What time is Danika's appointment today?" I asked Maya as I walked into the kitchen and saw her eating a bowl of cereal. Danika was sitting in her high chair, eating diced bananas and strawberries.

"Where did you come from?" Maya asked.

"The front door was unlocked," I said.

"Danika's appointment is at nine o'clock," Maya responded after chewing.

"Where's Jensen?" I asked as I noticed he was nowhere to be seen.

"Beach or cemetery," Maya said.

"Is he going to Danika's doctor's appointment?" I asked.

"I would assume. He's the one that made it," Maya said, looking at a framed picture.

"Wow, I remember that," I said, looking over her shoulder at the picture.

"You should. You both were fresh out of Eastlake at the time."

"Hi, baby blue eyes," I said, cooing and picking up Danika.

"You're just the sweetest little thing, aren't you?" I said as Danika jumped up and down, getting excited.

"Now, Dean, I just got her to settle down," Maya said frustrated.

"And we just went and messed all that up, didn't we?" I said, making fun and smiling as Danika giggled and smiled also. "Do you forgive us, Grandma?" I asked, holding Danika and looking at Maya with a sad face.

"I guess, but only because she's cute," Maya said. "Not you."

"We'll take that," I said, shaking my head up and down, "won't we?" while bouncing Danika up and down. "Now, what do you think? Should I go and find Daddy and light a fire under his bum or what?" I said, looking at Danika.

After setting Danika down in her high chair, I jumped in my truck and drove to the cemetery. As soon as I pulled up, I saw Jensen's truck parked by the curb outside the cemetery with his surfboard on the back. Parking behind him, I got out and noticed that the cemetery was closed. Looking in between the iron-barred gate surrounding the cemetery, I saw Jensen lying on the grass next to Octavia's headstone. Hopping over the gate, I walked up to him and saw tons of flowers all over her grave, along with cards and little signs that looked a bit aged and worn.

Some said, "RIP," while others said, "Gone too soon" and "Gone but never forgotten." It was beautiful to see how she was so loved and adored by her fans. Looking out across the cemetery, I saw someone that looked out of place, wearing a dark cloak that hid their face. I watched as it seemed to make eye contact with me, and I saw a faint red glow as if they were its eyes. Jogging up to the mausoleum to catch up to whoever that was, I came upon two large glass doors. Opening one of the glass doors, I walked in, and suddenly I was hit by an immensely cold breeze.

"Is anyone here?" I asked aloud.

Everything in the mausoleum was quiet when all of a sudden a lightning bolt flew at my face.

Dodging it, I went to flick my wrist and noticed that I was already holding my spear, looking at my attacker shadowed by a dark cloak.

"Do I know you?" I asked.

"You should," it said.

"You seem so familiar," I said. "Who are you?"

"I am your reflection," it said, revealing its face before attacking me again.

"Okay, that makes a lot of sense," I said confused. "If we are one and the same, why are we fighting?" I asked when suddenly I was stabbed in the side by its lightning bolt. Falling to the floor, I noticed that there was no one else in the room but me.

"Ah, this can't be happening," I said in pain.

Flicking my wrist, my spear vanished. Picking myself up off the floor, I walked out of the mausoleum and over to where Jensen was lying next to Octavia's headstone.

"If ever the jinn wanted to take you out, they wouldn't have to look far," I said, nudging Jensen to wake up after I'd walked up to him.

"What are you doing here, Dean?" Jensen asked, picking his head up.

"I'm checking on my friend," I said smiling. "You still have sand on your feet and your wet suit on. Wasn't it cold out here last night?" I asked as Jensen shrugged.

"Who'd you go and piss off now that you have blood on your clothes?" Jensen asked, ignoring my question and looking at the side of my shirt.

"I'm at war with myself," I said jokingly, but thinking to myself, *It's the truth.*

"Who won?" Jensen asked.

"Of course I did," I said, looking at Jensen oddly smiling.

"I can see," Jensen said, chuckling to himself.

"I remember the last time I was here," I said. "I was pulling you off Octavia's father. You almost killed that guy."

"I probably would have, had you not been there to stop me," Jensen said, taking a deep breath.

"I concur. But I'm sure his face is still hurting from that hit you gave him," I laughed. "So listen."

"What's up?"

"Octavia wouldn't want to see you like this," I said.

"Well, I guess it's good then she's not here anymore to see me," Jensen said, looking down and shaking his head.

"I can't begin to comprehend what you're going through, but if you let me in, I might understand. I might even be able to help you," I said sympathetically.

"I just keep playing it over and over in my head," Jensen said, gesturing a circle with his index finger, motioning his thoughts.

"There's nothing you could have done," I said. "It's been a year and a half, it's time you forgive yourself."

"It's so hard, Dean," Jensen said, beginning to break down in tears. "Every time I look at Danika, I'm reminded of Octavia," Jensen said, "and it kills me all over again."

"I said the same thing to Nathaniel once," I said thinking. "It's hard. You know what he told me?" I said, looking at Jensen and envisioning the time Nathaniel said it to me. *It's supposed to be, that's what makes life so thrilling.*

"The modern-day Yoda, wasn't he?" Jensen said and smiled, wiping his tears.

"I loved your dad as if he were my own," I said and smiled. "I only have the fondest of memories of him, even if he was like Yoda at times."

"Well, come on then. Let's get out of here," Jensen said, standing up.

"Hey, there's one more thing . . . ," I was saying when we were suddenly interrupted.

"Hey, you two!" a man shouted, walking up to us. "You know you're not supposed to be here before opening hours?"

"Sorry about that," I said as he looked at Octavia's headstone.

"She was a beautiful singer and a beautiful person," the man said. "I love the granite headstone that was chosen."

"Thank you," Jensen said politely.

"Wait a minute . . . you're her husband?" the man asked.

"Yeah."

"The way your wife touched the world with her kindness can never be matched," the man said.

"Thank you for those kind words. I appreciate it," Jensen said, shaking the man's hand.

"You're welcome. You boys make sure you drive home safe now," the man said before walking away.

***

Jensen

After driving home to pick up Danika, I saw my mom. She looked sad and appeared to be deep in thought.

"Hey, Mom," I said, walking up behind her and kissing her on the back of the head.

"Well, hello," Maya responded and smiled. "How are you?

"I'll be all right," I said.

"Perhaps a shower first before you leave?" Maya said, seeing that my feet were covered in sand and I was wearing board shorts.

"You're probably right," I said, going upstairs.

The Good Doctor

Jensen

Stepping out of the shower onto a soft, light-green mat, I almost slipped when it gave way from under me. Getting my balance, I couldn't help but laugh and think of Octavia and how she'd told me, *"We're going to have to get a new shower mat soon. I almost slipped on that one."*

Closing my eyes for just a moment, I went to a wonderful memory in my head.

"Don't you wish we could stay like this forever?" Octavia smiled.

"We'll always be like this, Octavia. I gave you my heart, and we'll be tethered together, forever."

"I love you, Jensen."

"I love you, Octavia."

Opening my eyes, tears filled them as I gasped.

"I miss you so much," I said softly to myself, shaking my head, trying not to cry.

After getting dressed, I went downstairs and got Danika ready to go to her pediatrician appointment. Putting her in her car seat, Dean hopped in the truck with us, and we sped off.

Walking into a waiting room that was painted baby blue and had stickers on the walls of all kinds of Disney characters, I looked up at the TV overhead to see it was playing the movie *Brave*. There were many chairs for people to sit on, a couple small tables with magazines and coloring books fanned out, and a vase with fake flowers in it. While filling out a bunch of paperwork, I saw that Danika was watching the movie intensely as Tigist sat between her legs and watched it with her. They both seemed to love the part when Merida was fighting off a big mean bear. Then a nurse called us to the back. Tigist disappeared, and Danika began to cry. I picked her up to soothe her, and she stopped crying when I began rubbing her back.

"Can you undress her to her diaper and put her on the scale please?" a kind nurse asked.

"Yes," I responded, taking to her instructions then placing Danika on the scale.

"She's 19 pounds, eight ounces," the nurse said.

"Is that good?" Dean asked.

"She's right where she needs to be," the nurse said. "You have the prettiest eyes, sweetheart," the nurse said, patting Danika on the cheek.

"You guys will be in room 11. The doctor will be with you shortly."

Room 11 had posters on the walls explaining all about germs and the importance of protecting yourself and others around you from viruses.

"Hello, how are we doing today?" a doctor said, walking into the room. "I'm Dr. Tuck."

"Jensen Kane," I said, shaking her hand.

"Everybody knows you," she said, smiling and possibly flirting. "Embrace the Fate is one of my all-time favorite bands."

"I'm glad to hear that. Thank you so much," Dean said, smiling and introducing himself. "I'm Dean."

"I know who you are too. You're only the greatest drummer in the world," Dr. Tuck said as she and Dean exchanged smiles.

"That's what they say," Dean said cockily.

"And what's your name?" she said, looking at Danika.

"Dude, she's hot," Dean whispered in my ear and smiled. "I think she likes me."

"Her name is Danika," I said, answering her and ignoring Dean. But he nudged me and gave me a smile and a thumbs-up.

"Say, Dr. Tuck," Dean said confidently, "there's a party at my house tonight. I think you should come," draping his arm around her.

"Mr. Rouge," Dr. Tuck said, "if I didn't know any better, I would say you're hitting on me."

"Listen, Dr. Tuck, I find any girl who surfs attractive," Dean said politely.

"How do you know I surf?" Dr. Tuck asked.

"Dr. Tuck, it's as clear as day," Dean said. "I saw the surfboard in your office. Here's my address. The party starts at eight," Dean said and smiled.

"Well, thank you. I'll try to make it," she said, smiling at me and taking the address from Dean's hand.

"So, Danika," Dr. Tuck said, "let's take a look at you . . . Have her eyes always moved from side to side so quickly like this?" Dr. Tuck asked, looking closely at Danika's eyes with a medical apparatus.

"No, it just started about a week ago. That's why I made the appointment," I said.

"She appears to be having trouble focusing," Dr. Tuck said as she took an examining tool with a light and a microscope and closely looked into each of Danika's eyes.

"The eye movements she's displaying are common signs of blindness, and she doesn't seem to be sensitive to light, which calls for concern," Dr. Tuck said. "But there's no way to know for sure without sending her to an optometrist."

"Blindness?" I said confused.

"That doesn't make sense," Dean added.

"I have the number of the optometrist that I've worked with before," Dr. Tuck said softly.

"He can run some tests," she said. "Then we'll know for sure."

"I understand," I said, deep in thought.

Dean

Jumping in the truck, we started on our way home. When we left the doctor's office, Jensen didn't say much, but I could tell he had a lot on his mind. I was unsure about how he felt about the possibility that Danika could be blind.

"What are you thinking, Jensen?" I asked.

"I'm thinking, there has to be a reason for her blindness," Jensen said. "There has to be."

"My god, what if she never learns to surf?" I said sadly.

"That's your biggest concern?" Jensen asked, looking at me

weird.

"Dear god, yes," I said passionately. "Surfing the ocean is the closest to heaven anyone could ever be. It's like a religion. What are you thinking?"

"I think Danika sees through Tigist's eyes. She was watching the movie *Brave* at the doctor's office perfectly, and the second Tigist left, Danika began to cry. This has happened many times before, I just never put it together till now. She doesn't need an optometrist, there's nothing wrong with her."

"But how long will she have to rely on Tigist for her eyes?" I asked.

"I don't know," Jensen replied.

"Are you still coming to the party tonight?" I asked as we pulled up to the house.

"Yeah, man," Jensen said as I began to get out of the truck.

"I've gotta get going," I said stretching.

"Where?" Jensen asked.

"Home. I have a party to plan and people to call to make it happen," I said. "I'm thinking . . . a taco truck. Make sure he brings you little one," I said, kissing Danika on the cheek as she cooed. "Love you, sweet girl," I told her before walking away.

"Wait, you mean there was no party?" Jensen asked.

"Hell no! That was a spur-of-the moment thing, to get the good doctor to come out and hang."

"What makes you think she'll come?" Jensen asked.

"She's a surfer girl, Jensen. The one thing all surfer girls have in common . . . is they all love to party. Hell, we should do some night surfing too."

Jensen

As night came, I wondered if Dean's invite to the good doctor had worked and if she'd indeed show up to the party.

"What's up, man?" Dean said, opening the door after I rang the bell.

"Nothing," I said and grinned.

"Did you bring your board?" Dean asked.

"I did," I smiled. "It's in the garage."

"You know the code to my garage?" Dean asked awkwardly.

"I know a lot of things," I said, looking at Dean.

"Where's Danika?" Dean asked.

"Mom's got her. They'll be over soon," I replied.

"Cool," Dean said, closing the door. "You want a beer?"

"Yes please," I said when I saw the new bar Dean had put into his house. "Damn! Did you ever think we'd have it so good after we got out of Eastlake?" I asked and smiled as Dean handed me a beer.

"Dude, before you even showed up there, I was unsure I'd even survive that place," Dean said, tipping his bottle of Modelo.

"Cheers," I replied, looking at a picture on the wall. "Is that Bran Castle?"

"It is," Dean said.

"You still own it?" I asked.

"Yes," Dean replied.

"Does it still give you the creeps?"

"More than you know. I'm looking into making it a museum now. Connor is there right now with his girlfriend, Anna. He has a bit more knowledge with that museum stuff since he just made Neverland Ranch a museum," Dean said as the doorbell rang.

When people started arriving, it was around eight. Dean had really gone all out from getting a taco truck to an open bar. Like my home, Dean's also had a staircase from his backyard that would go directly onto the sand on the beach. People started going down to the beach as the house filled up. Some even began going into the water to surf. Then the doorbell rang, and Dean answered it. It was Dr. Tuck, but she wasn't alone. The man she was with was wearing board shorts, sandals, and a Quicksilver T-shirt. He was white with bleached hair, tanned skin, and had an attitude to go with it, and he seemed already a bit drunk.

"Dr. Tuck," Dean said, giving her a hug, "who's your friend?"

"Please call me Nikki. This is my boyfriend, Shawn."

"And here I thought you were single and I'd have you all to myself," Dean said.

"That's pretty bold," Nikki said.

"Life's too short not to be bold. When I see something or someone I like, I go for it," Dean said. "Well, come on in," Dean said politely as Shawn looked to have an attitude.

"Where's the bar, rock star?" Shawn said, stumbling inside

and pushing Dean out of the way.

"Help yourself, Shawn," Dean said chuckling. "Classy guy."

"I'm sorry, we were at another party before this, and he had a little too much to drink," Nikki said.

"See, I knew you were a party girl," Dean said, taking her hand and bringing her inside smiling.

Nikki

As Dean showed me his house, I spotted Jensen outside, looking at the ocean. I was not sure why, but I felt such a connection with him.

"So I thought I'd see Danika here?" I asked, walking up to Jensen.

"She was here earlier with my mother, but it was getting late," Jensen said before something in the house spilled and broke.

"So I was thinking, after you left my office this afternoon, I felt a real bond and closeness between Danika and I. I wanted to let you know that whenever my schedule does not meet yours, I will come see her at your home, or you can bring her to mine, if that would be all right?" I asked, handing Jensen my card, with my phone number and home address on the back.

"That would be fine," Jensen said. He and I locked eyes and for a moment, and I felt a strong connection. "Do you watch over all your patients this closely?" Jensen added.

"No," I smiled ever so slightly.

"Listen, Mr. Rock Star, I know your wife is dead. But are you trying to close in on my girl?" Shawn said, walking out from the house even more drunk than when he arrived.

Slurring his words and almost falling face-first onto the ground, he proceeded to get in Jensen's face.

"Okay, Shawn, you're drunk," I said. "I'm sorry, we were at another party before this, Jensen, and he had one too many drinks."

"What are you apologizing for?" Shawn said rudely, looking at me.

"Got a bit of an overprotective vibe there, don't you?" Jensen commented.

"What the hell's going on here?" Dean said, walking up.

"There's the other big shot that wants to do my girl," Shawn said, directing his anger toward Dean.

"Oh my god, please shut up, Shawn!" I said before Shawn pushed me.

Without any hesitation, Jensen punched Shawn, and he fell to the ground like a sack of potatoes.

"Jensen, he's knocked out cold," Dean said and laughed. "I love it!"

"Are you okay?" Jensen asked.

"I'm all right."

"Has he ever pushed you before?" Dean asked.

"No, that was the first and the last," I said, shaking my head.

"Jensen, you broke his nose," another one of the party goers said laughing.

Laying him down in the back seat of my car, Jensen went with me to dump Shawn off at his home, and then we went back to Dean's house. Not long after we arrived back at the party, we went out into the ocean for some night surfing. I could tell as I watched that Jensen and Dean were no strangers to night surfing. As the rest of the night went by like a blur, I enjoyed every minute I spent with Jensen.

Love Found

Nikki

Months passed, and Jensen and I became very close. Shawn, my ex-boyfriend, didn't care for this and began stalking me. He'd follow me wherever I'd go, and I could feel his dark, sad presence everywhere. One day I spotted him at the grocery store; he became very pushy and wanted answers for things that were none of his business. Fearing that he could become violent, I got a restraining order. This angered him to a point where he became relentless, and odd things began happening around my house. Sometimes the electricity to my house would just shut off. When I'd go out to investigate, I would find that someone went inside my breaker box and just shut them all off. I even got a lock for the breaker box, but before long it was happening again because he cut the lock. I always felt better when I talked to Jensen about what Shawn was doing. Jensen thought that in time, Shawn would stop. I loved seeing Jensen so much that when he was around, I'd get goose bumps. I just wondered at times if he had the same feelings toward me. At times I felt like he was holding back feelings in fear of not wanting to get too close. I totally understood since he'd lost Octavia.

One evening I was expecting Jensen for dinner. As I was driving back from the grocery store, an eerie feeling came over as I pulled into the garage. I saw the garage door going into my house was slightly open. Getting out of the car, I walked inside.

"How was your day at work, honey?" a man asked as I walked in the house.

"How did you get in here?" I asked, frightened when I saw

Shawn in the kitchen cutting some carrots on a cutting board.

"You really should wait for your garage to close all the way before you leave," he said. "And you disabled the alarm," he continued. "That probably isn't very smart, considering any jerk could just walk in—"

"Any jerk did just walk in," I said mad. "You shouldn't be here," I said, frustrated and scared.

"Ah, but I disagree," he said, explaining himself. "See, I think you've spent enough time alone, and maybe now you can see the light," he said, showing me the knife in his hand.

"I didn't say I needed time, Shawn. I told you we were over," I said, shaking my head. "Leave now! I'm expecting someone."

"Oh, baby, I'm not going anywhere," he said, shaking his head no and waving the kitchen knife back and forth. "Who are you expecting?"

"That's none of your business," I said, trying not to show any fear.

"Why are you doing this to me, Nikki?" he asked, becoming emotionally unstable.

"Why am I doing this to you?" I asked frustrated.

"I thought you just needed time to process," Shawn said.

"Time to process?" I laughed. "Process what? You're creepy as hell," I said, walking into the living room. "Leave now, before I call the police," I said, turning to pick up the phone. "Unless you want to add domestic abuse to your résumé?" I continued, becoming scared, when he suddenly grabbed me by the arm. "Let me go," I said, looking down at his hand on my arm and the knife in his other hand.

"You're really going to trash our relationship?" Shawn asked, confused.

"Shawn, it's been a year," I said, looking at him. "I still get your creepy letters. I still feel your presence watching me at the grocery store. I've even seen your car sitting up the street just watching my house," I said with a disgusted look on my face. "Enough is enough, Shawn," I said. "You have serious issues. Now get the hell out of my house!"

Suddenly he grabbed my shirt and threw me to the ground. Lunging at me as I was on the floor, he began trying to rip the clothes from my body before I kneed him in his crown jewels, and he fell to the floor beside me. As he lay on the floor growling in pain, I quickly got up, grabbed the phone, and locked myself in the bathroom, calling 911.

"Do you see what you make me do, Nikki?" he shouted, kicking the door in, but not before I had called 911.

While he was holding the knife up to me, the doorbell rang.

"Who the hell is that?" Shawn said, grabbing me by the neck, holding the knife to my face, and threatening to kill me if I made any noises.

"Look what we have here, if it ain't Mr. Rock Star," Shawn said, looking through the peephole.

"Shawn, why don't you open the door, I already know you're in there," Jensen said from the other side of the door.

Quickly opening the door, Shawn pointed the knife to Jensen's throat, just barely scraping it. Grabbing Jensen by the collar, he pulled him into the house very carefully.

"Please don't hurt him, Shawn," I said crying.

"Listen, Shawn," Jensen said, gently pushing the knife away from his throat, "I'm not normal, man. I'll smack you right in the face whether you're holding a knife or not," smacking Shawn in the mouth. "In all fairness, Shawn, I think I should share with you—" Jensen said before he was cut off as Shawn buried the knife into his stomach.

I watched in horror as Shawn stabbed Jensen repeatedly. As Shawn backed away, Jensen fell to the floor.

"Now, what to do with you?" Shawn said, steering his attention toward me.

"Boy, that hurts," Jensen said, taking a deep breath and picking himself up off the floor. "You should have let me finish my sentence."

"How . . . ? What . . . ?" Shawn said as I looked on in shock. "I . . . ," Shawn stammered, scared out of his mind as the police pulled up outside.

"Looks like your escorts have arrived," Jensen said as he put his hand on Shawn's shoulder. "I know the questions you must have," Jensen looked at Shawn, pretending to sympathize.

"I'll tell the police what you are," Shawn said in fear, threatening Jensen.

"You could, but would they listen?" Jensen said, taking

a deep breath. "Don't ever come around Nicole again, do you understand?"

"Yes," Shawn said, frightened.

***

"Why is it, Jensen, that I find you involved in a lot more stuff than I probably should?" a man asked, walking up to Jensen.

"Detective Winters," Jensen said, "how long has it been?"

"Since Eastlake," Winters said coldly. "You know, your luck is going to run out sooner or later. I just hope I'm there when it does."

"I'll keep that in mind, " Jensen said condescendingly.

"You know, ma'am, you should be more careful of who you spend your time with," Winters said, looking at me. "You know, Jensen, we still have no idea what happened to that Jane Doe after the Eastlake incident," Winters said, looking at Jensen this time, implying he had something to do with someone's disappearance.

"Are we done, Detective?" Jensen asked. "Or should I call my lawyer?" Jensen said, taking a jab. "You remember my lawyer, don't you? Pierce Hatchet."

"Watch yourself, Jensen," Detective Winters said, walking past me.

"What is he talking about?" I asked, looking at Jensen.

"Ignore him," Jensen said. "He's just angry he's not better at his job."

"Are you okay?" I asked, touching Jensen's stomach. "I thought he stabbed you."

"There are things I think you need to know about me," Jensen said, taking my hand after the cops took Shawn into custody and we walked up to the doorstep of my house.

"Would you like to stay?" I asked smiling.

"If that's what you want," Jensen smiled as I turned on some music. "Blake Shelton," Jensen said.

"You don't like Blake Shelton?" I asked.

"I'm more of a Misfits, Bad Religion, Godsmack kinda guy," Jensen said, shaking his head smiling.

"Would you like to?" I asked, extending my hand out, inviting him to slow-dance with me.

As he and I swayed from side to side, I could feel the closeness of our bodies create heat. I began feeling his nervousness, afraid he might be getting too close. I moved closer and rested my head on his chest, and he put his hands on my hips. I could sense his presence while he smelled my hair as if he were breathing me in.

"I'm really glad you're here," I said, looking up at Jensen.

"I'm happy to be here," Jensen smiled as I looked up at him.

"I love you," I told Jensen, looking into his eyes as the song was coming to its end.

Looking at me with no words, he moved closer, and our lips met one another.

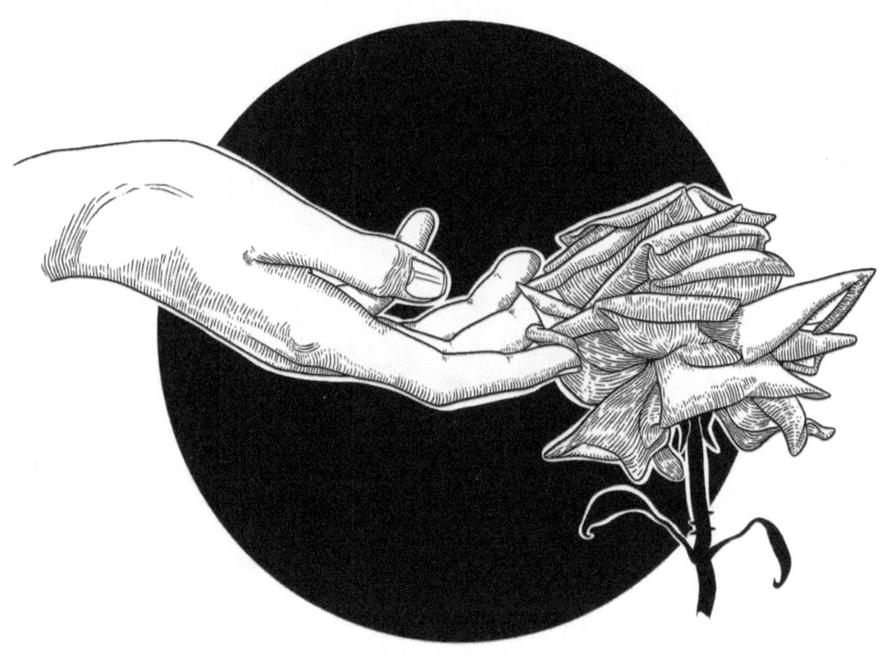

New Future Weapon

Danika

When I was three, my father married Nicole Tuck. Their wedding was beautiful, and I participated as their flower girl and ring bearer. Their love for one another was beautiful. When I turned five, I was well versed in the martial arts after following the teachings of my father and grandmother. I was taught to rely on my other senses—smell, hearing, and that sixth sense that only some people had. My father and Nikki taught me to surf at a very young age and to rely on Tigist as my eyes. Growing up with Nikki as my mother was wonderful. I loved her very much, and she had been there for me throughout all my trials and tribulations. But not a day passed that I didn't think about my real mother, Octavia. My father told me so many beautiful stories about her, and at times I felt as if I did know her. I knew she was overwhelmingly talented in multiple things, but I often wondered if I'd ever measure up as a singer, as it was my dream to follow in her footsteps and achieve the same success.

My father turned to the elder grimoire for guidance, improving his katana defense and combat skills. He taught himself gun kata through the teachings of Rowlis and Zamael and learned to incorporate it into his fighting style. His style had become extremely unique and dominant when he learned the martial art pencak silat. By the time I was twelve, my hand-to-hand combat methods had evolved fully and surpassed anything my father or grandmother had ever seen, and at a young age my father found his equal when sparring against me. He always said, *"One day when you have sight. There will be nothing that could stop you.*" As a child there were many jinn and reapers that tried to take my life. They were an unrelenting force that were harder to kill and were better versed on martial arts and using melee weapons. But with every attempt, they always failed.

When I turned fourteen, my school told my parents that continuing my middle school education would be a waste of time as I had been an honor roll student since kindergarten and exceeded in everything academically. The school had an IQ test done, and I scored higher than Albert Einstein. His IQ test revealed a 160 score, and mine was 165.

At this time my father had been extremely active within the US military for years and had been a master sergeant for the elite Delta Force team Zero. I remember Nikki becoming very upset about his decision to join the Delta Force team Zero as he was putting himself right into the middle of all the weak-minded fools who followed the jinn.

His decision to join Delta Force team Zero came at a time when terrorist groups were on the rise in the Middle East, and a specific one was boasting all sorts of claims and threats that made news headlines. They called themselves Khatia Dafie. The group was formed of jinn disguised as humans and weak-minded humans that were less than men. It was said that the group lived and died by the writing within the Quran. It was like a thief in the night when they rose to superpower and began threatening the world. It was on my father's fourth tour that he killed another one of their generals, and a bounty was put on him for $20,000 dead or $90,000 alive. When this happened, my Uncle Dean joined the Delta Force team Zero alongside my father to help watch his back.

This was also the time in my life when I discovered that I was gay. I found women more sexually appealing than men, it was something about their soft, feminine voices and their soft skin. I had only had two girlfriends up to this time in my life and my grandmother wasn't happy about my being gay. She'd often chastise me and say *"you're living in sin. Walk in the light God and Jesus set fourth."* When I met Valerie, it was as if time stood still. I knew I loved her the moment I saw her. Tigist told me to not be ashamed and that it was okay to have these feelings. But I often questioned what my ancestor Jesus quoted in the Bible, wherein he says:

"If a man lies with a male as with a woman, they have committed an abomination; the two of them shall be put to death."

This verse has always stayed with me. But my feelings never changed, and I longed for the day to see everything for myself with my own eyes and touch a woman's skin and watch myself do it. I could tell I was very beautiful as I would often see myself through Tigist's eyes and touch my nude body in front of a mirror and be in complete fascination. I prayed for a miracle, anything that could cure my blindness so I might see. I hated living in darkness, but I was also very blessed to have Tigist.

***

"Nikki?" I asked as I walked out of our downstairs bathroom.

"How did you know I was here? I'm not even close to you," Nikki responded.

"I hear everything, and I smell the faint aroma of the Acqua de Gio Dad gave you for Christmas," I said and smiled.

"Is Valerie picking you up today?" Nikki asked.

"No. She's surfing first period today. Bastian is picking me up instead. He should be here any minute," I said. "Are you okay?" I asked, concerned when I heard Nikki take a deep breath.

"I just saw on the news, the riots in the Middle East are becoming worse, and Khatia Dafie is demanding that the US turn over the Reaper of Fallujah."

"Ah, you know Dad, he'll be okay," I said.

"I know, but your father has that gift of pissing people off to an extreme," Nikki said nervously as I grabbed my walking stick and backpack. "Have a great day at school, sweetheart," Nikki said, kissing me on the back of the head. "And, Danika, no getting into it with that girl today," Nikki added in a serious tone as I grabbed my coat from the closet by the back door.

"I know, Nikki," I said.

"I mean it, young lady," she said firmly. "You have a ton of your father in you . . . and that also scares me," she continued under her breath.

"You mean it every time you say it, Nikki," I said, walking into the kitchen, "and I heard that last part."

"Of course you did."

"Hey, you," Grandma said before I turned around and ran into her.

"Hey, Grandma," I said, giving her a hug.

"So aware of your surroundings. But you didn't even know I was here," Grandma said.

"I wouldn't go as far as saying that," I said before walking past her and out the front door.

"I overheard you and Danika talking," Maya said softly. "Jensen will be all right, Nikki."

"I know," Nikki said, pausing. "I'm going to take a shower and then head to the office," Nikki said.

"I'll be in the front yard gardening," Maya said, feeling her back pockets to find her gardening gloves she just had.

Walking down the entryway, I could hear the birds, bees, and the slow gust of wind that howled. I could smell rain in the air. Suddenly I heard the front door shut.

"Now where'd I leave my gloves?" Maya said to herself, looking around.

"Looking for these, Grandma?" I said, handing her the gloves and smiling.

"So when did you take these from my pocket?" Grandma asked, looking at me.

"When we were in the kitchen, before you questioned whether I paid attention to my surroundings," I said as my grandma smiled and I handed her the gloves.

In the wind I smelled Grandma's perfume, red velvet; it was her favorite. It was a strong but soothing scent, relaxing but exotic. I could smell the herbs she was planting in the garden. But my favorites were the red roses that surrounded our perimeter fence. Their smell was intoxicating, till I'd smell one that was on its way to meet death, and today was one of those days. I'd caught the scent of a dying rose on the breeze. After finding it, I walked over to it and gently touched its petals with my fingertips.

"It's not your time, little one," I whispered, continuing to touch it with the tips of my fingers.

"Hey, Danika!" Bastian said, walking up to the outside of our fence.

"You startled me, Bastian," I said, pulling my fingers away from the rose.

"That's funny, usually you can sense when someone's coming," Bastian said as I opened the gate.

"Well, today I didn't," I said sassing. "I thought you were picking me up in your car?"

"Speeding ticket," Bastian said disappointed. "My parents grounded me."

"That sucks," I said. "City bus then?"

"City bus," Bastian repeated, confirming.

"I hope you never speed with my granddaughter in the car," Grandma said, walking up behind me.

"Never, Ms. Kane," Bastian said quickly.

"Good," she responded, looking at Bastian. "You two best be on your way," she said, kissing me on the cheek.

"I love you, Grandma," I said before walking off with Bastian.

Maya

Turning around, I looked at the dying rose and heard Danika's voice in the wind:

"Let there be life," she said faintly.

I watched as the rose blossomed back to life.

Danika

"Hey, are you okay, Danika?" Bastian asked as we walked.

"Yeah, I think Nikki's pregnant," I said, holding on to Bastian's arm.

"How can you tell?" Bastian asked.

"I just can," I said.

"Are you more in tune to stuff because you're blind?" Bastian asked.

"Rude!" I said frustrated, looking in his direction. "It's not a blind thing. I just feel things."

"Well, it's creepy. You remember a couple years ago when I was out for a two weeks from school because I got that Covid 19, crap?"

"Yeah," I said listening.

"If I recall correctly, you told me at school that I was coming down with something and that I should listen to you because you're never wrong."

"Yes, and I was right?" I asked.

"It's creepy. You know, now that I think about it, I didn't get better until you came to my house to see me," Bastian said thinking. "Does Valerie know how creepy you are?"

"What can I say, I'm the new future weapon against anything evil," I said, making fun. "And Valerie appreciates that I sense things sooner than everyone else."

"Covid 19 that was pretty scary stuff," Bastian said as we walked up to the bus stop.

"Makes you wonder doesn't it?" I said thinking.

"Wonder what?"

"If something like a virus will take part in ending the world."

"How was the seventeenth birthday?" Bastian asked changing the conversation.

"My birthday was good, it was basic. Nothing over the top exciting—just me, Mom, Dad, and Grandma," I said as the city bus pulled up to the stop.

"Does she need help?" the driver asked Bastian as he got on first.

"I haven't lost the use of my ears," I said annoyed as Bastian stood on the first step of the bus.

"I apologize. Why don't you come aboard," the driver said.

"No, thank you," I said, getting a bad feeling. "I'll walk."

"You'll be late, Danika," Bastian said, confused about me walking.

"I'm okay with that," I said, turning and walking away. "Thank you."

"Danika, what's wrong?" Bastian asked, jumping off the bus.

"Nothing, I'm fine. I just need some time to myself."

"Clearly, something's wrong, Danika. What is it?"

"I can't keep the door open forever, and we have to go. So are you going with her or staying on the bus?" the driver asked, annoyed and rolling his eyes.

"I'm getting off," Bastian said.

"No, Bastian, get on the bus, get to school. I'll get there. I just need this time to myself."

"Are you sure?" Bastian asked again.

"Yeah, just go," I said. "I'll be fine."

As soon as Bastian walked in, the driver closed the door. I could feel his gaze upon me. As they pulled away from the curb and began driving down the street, I knelt down and pretended to tie my shoe. Standing back up, I folded up my walking stick and put it in my backpack. Kneeling back down, I put my fist to the ground and shot off like a rocket into the sky.

You know how I feel when you do this, Danika, Tigist said in my head in an chastising tone. *Anyone could have seen you.*

"Did you feel the dark energy coming off the bus driver, Tigist?" I asked, ignoring Tigist's warnings.

I felt it. He's not a jinn though, Tigist said.

"Yeah, I only sensed darkness," I said confused. "Why only darkness, Tigist?"

Search your feelings, Danika, Tigist said as I focused.

"He's responsible for many evil things," I said as the wind blew in my face. "I can sense it. We should do something about it."

What do you want to do, Danika? Drop out of school and become a superhero? Tigist asked sarcastically. *Fight crime?*

"What's wrong with that?" I asked and smiled.

Not on my watch, young one. All the great superheroes went to school, Tigist said. *Just remember that darkness you felt coming from the driver. Don't ignore it, and always be wary of how far you reach into understanding that darkness. That darkness belongs to the dark lord,* Tigist said.

"What could happen if I dove too deep into the darkness?" I asked.

The darkness could trap you there.

"Well, I'm already in darkness. How much worse can it get?" I said jokingly.

Don't joke, Danika. Your blindness doesn't come without reason, Tigist said.

"I know, it shields me from the jinn and keeps me hidden."

So you do listen to everything I say.

"I have to. You get really mad at me when I don't. Now let's fly and enjoy ourselves."

Why do I feel that this bus driver thing was just an excuse to fly? We should've walked.

"Yeah well, coulda, woulda, shoulda," I smiled, extending

my right arm out. "Now break away, Tigist," I said as I flicked my wrist, and Tigist came flying out from my hand. "You can see everything from up here, Tigist."

Seeing everything through Tigist's eyes was so beautiful. We were flying through the clouds together, doing dips and rolls and sidewinders, pushing it harder than usual in my flight, when suddenly there was a loud *boom*!

Danika, you broke the sound barrier! Tigist shouted excitedly.

"It feels so good to let loose, doesn't it, Tigist?" I asked excitedly.

I love the sky, Danika, Tigist said as she swooped in and out of the clouds. *I love it!*

Slowing down, we came to a mountain range. I stopped and levitated, looking down at the mountains.

"Isn't it beautiful, Tigist?"

I know what you're thinking, Danika. Let's not do that, Tigist said, closing her eyes. *That's a bad idea.*

"You think by closing your eyes, Tigist, you're going to stop me?"

I was kinda hoping, maybe.

"I'll do it blind, Tigist," I said condescendingly.

I wouldn't put it past you, Tigist said, opening her eyes and looking at the mountain. *Reckless child!*

"Come on, Tigist. Let's live a little."

Flying through a mountain is not my idea of living a little.

Flying off in the opposite direction of the mountain, I then turned around and flew as fast as I could toward the middle of a huge mountain, grabbing Tigist along the way.

Danika, we're not doing this! Tigist shouted as I flicked my wrist and Tigist disappeared. *Danika, this isn't safe to do if you can't see!* Tigist said as I continued to fly toward the mountain.

"Nope. But it's going to be fun."

165 IQ, my foot. Albert Einstein would have never done something so dumb.

When I hit the mountain, rock and debris flew everywhere. As we came out the opposite side, I flicked my wrist, and Tigist came flying out.

"Holy . . ." I said before Tigist interrupted.

Watch your mouth, young lady, Tigist said.

"Tigist, we just flew through a mountain," I said excitedly, twirling in the air. "Did you feel the rocks hit us? It felt like we flew through a pile of leaves."

Yes, child, we've established that you are indeed reckless, Tigist said, shaking her head.

"Reckless or not, that was awesome," I said, smiling and levitating to the sky. "I'm awesome."

Ah yes, super fun. Speaking of fun . . . , Tigist said cheekily, *I do believe you have school.*

"I know, let's go."

Levitating over to my school, I looked down and saw the bus stop that was close to our school.

"Tigist, stay up here and fly," I said. "Find me later!" I shouted, flying down to the school.

Landing behind the bleachers on the football field, I knelt down to get my cane from my backpack and walked out from behind the bleachers.

"Well, look who it is! Q-tip, what's going on?" I heard a girl say, laughing with her friends.

"Funny. You should leave the comedy to the professionals. Would you say to someone in a wheelchair, 'Nice Go-Kart'?"

"Well . . . yeah," one of them said, laughing once more.

"Okay, now I understand what I'm dealing with," I said, swinging my cane and almost hitting one of them in the face.

"Watch it with the pool cue. Just because you and Valerie are queers doesn't mean you get a free pass on an ass-whooping."

"Gosh, it would have been a shame to hit a piece of plastic off your face," I said, walking past them.

"Halloween is coming soon, retard. Stay mouthy, and you'll see where it gets you," one of them said as I turned my back and walked away.

***

"Well, hello," I said, walking up to the bus stop casually.

"How did you get here already?" Bastian said, getting off the bus.

"I flew."

"Seriously. How did you get here already?" the bus driver

asked, looking at me oddly.

"Don't let your mind fantasize too deeply, bus driver. I've seen your mind, not good," I said, looking at the driver before turning and walking away with Bastian.

"Really though, Danika, how did you get here so fast?" Bastian asked as I just looked in his direction and smiled.

Young Lovers

Valerie

After an early-morning session of surf practice, I got to class, and all I could think about was the ocean and Danika. I was sitting for an hour through music class, and on my way out the door, Mr. Dupree stopped me.

"Do you have a moment to talk?" Mr. Dupree asked.

"Sure, Mr. Dupree, what's up?"

"Listen, Valerie, Juilliard is very interested in you. I think you have a real shot here at being accepted into their orchestra," Mr. Dupree said.

"Juilliard? Oh my god, really? Thank you so much, Mr. Dupree."

"Now I can't make any promises, but the orchestra is looking for only two celloists to give scholarships to."

"How did this happen? I thought you had to send in an application to get accepted," I asked.

"When you competed at the state finals last year, there was a Juilliard scout there, and she loved your solo piece," Mr. Dupree said.

After I heard this, I sped out of class to meet Danika before third period.

"Hey, baby," Danika said after I opened the door to walk out of class.

"How did you know it was me, beautiful?" I asked, smiling as Danika was leaning up against some lockers across from me.

"Cherry blossom shampoo, tea tree mint body wash. It's exhilarating, and no one else in school smells so pretty," Danika said flirtatiously.

"Have you been inside my shower?" I asked flirtatiously.

"Not yet," Danika whispered into my ear.

"All right, I guess I'll just keep walking," Bastian said, walking up behind Danika.

"See you later, Bastian," I said and smiled.

"Bye," Danika said as she hugged me.

"What class are you on your way to, babe?" I asked, kissing Danika on the lips.

"Horticulture," Danika answered as she gently placed her hands on my face.

"Mr. Dickman, he has a fun class," I said. "You're so beautiful," I said, fixated on every detail of Danika's face.

"Thank you," Danika said as she felt the smile on my face and smiled back.

"Your hair is wet," Danika said as soon as she felt my hair. "How were the waves this morning?"

"Excellent! I beat another one of your mom's records this morning," I said and smiled.

"She'd be proud," Danika said as the bell rang. "You have something to tell me," Danika said touching my face.

"How do you know?" I asked.

"I can sense it in your aura, you're excited," Danika said, smiling ever so slightly.

"I'm so excited, Danika. I'll walk you to class and explain."

"But you'll be late to your next class," Danika said.

"You're worth being late for," I said and kissed Danika. She held on to my arm, and I walked with her to class, explaining everything about Juilliard to her and what Mr. Dupree said about state finals last year and the scout from Juilliard.

***

I thought about Danika all day in class and thought of how proud she was of me for being considered to go to Juilliard. She was so beautiful and such a wonderful person. I felt so blessed to have her in my life. But today was different. I couldn't get her off my mind. I thought about the way she touched my face this morning.

It was as if she was trying to memorize every inch. When class was over, I walked to the cafeteria to meet Danika.

"Yo, Valerie!" a friend of mine said, walking up behind me.

"What's up, Matt?" I asked turning around.

"Listen, I remember you saying your parents are out of town this weekend, and I had to cancel the party tonight because my parents are staying in town," Matt said.

"Yes, we can use my house. Eight o'clock, right?" I asked, seeing Danika sit down at a table with Bastian.

"Yeah," Matt said, seeing that I was focused on Danika. "You should just tell her you love her already."

"Is it that obvious?" I asked, looking at Matt.

"She's all you ever talk about at surf practice," Matt said. "It's obvious."

Walking up behind Danika, I draped myself around her, kissing her neck and the back of her head.

"What's up, Bastian?" I said and smiled.

"Same old. What's up with you?" Bastian asked.

"You know the party we were going to tonight at Matt's house?"

"Yeah," Bastian said.

"Well, the plans changed. The party's at my house now," I said.

"Cool. I have something I want to talk to you about tonight," Danika said.

"That's good because I too have something to talk to you about," I said, hugging Danika tight.

"Well then, that settles it. We'll have our conversation tonight?" Danika said as I kissed her on the neck. "I'll see you tonight," Danika said, biting her lower lip before kissing me one last time.

"I can't wait," I whispered in her ear.

Danika

"What do you think she wants to talk about?" I asked Bastian.

"I don't know. What do you want to talk to her about?" Bastian asked.

"I'm going to tell her I love her," I responded. "I just hope she feels the same."

"She does," Bastian said reassuringly.

"How do you know?"

"I've seen the way she always looks at you. She loves you more than anything."

"I'm so happy, Bastian," I said, taking a deep breath and sighing.

***

"So this party you're going to tonight," Nikki asked as she braided my hair into one single dutch braid, "is Valerie picking you up?"

"Yeah," I responded.

"I really like Valerie," Nikki said.

"I'm glad," I said.

"I'm happy for you, Danika," Nikki said.

"I love her, Nikki," I said.

"That's great," Nikki responded.

"Do you think Grandma will ever understand and be happy for me?"

"I don't know, but I can tell you this. You can't help whom you love, and never let anyone tell you whom you can and can't love," Nikki said, taking a deep breath. "You understand?"

"Yeah," I responded. "Can I ask you something?"

"Anything," Nikki responded.

"Are you pregnant?" I asked.

"Yes," Nikki said with a big smile.

"What will you name the baby?" I asked.

"If it's a girl, I'd like to name her Trinity, and if it's a boy, Samuel."

"Those are both beautiful names," I asked standing up. "How do I look?"

"Absolutely breathtaking, my love," Nikki said as the doorbell rang.

"Well, hello, Valerie," I heard my grandma say.

"How are you, Ms. Kane?" Valerie asked as I walked up behind my grandma.

"I'm good, Valerie. Danika tells me you beat another one of Octavia's surfing records today and you may be attending

Juilliard after you graduate?" Grandma asked.

"Yeah, it's really cool, I got my name on another plaque on the wall next to my idol. But possibly being accepted into Juilliard, that's just a dream come true," Valerie said before I walked up to her and we walked out the door.

"Well, you girls have fun," Nikki said, saying goodbye.

"When is your grandma going to get over the fact that you're gay?" Valerie asked as we got in her Mustang and drove off.

"She always has this disappointed look on her face. Maybe she'll be over it around the time you tell your parents about us," I said.

"Yeah, my parents will disown me," Valerie responded.

"Is Bastian at the party yet?" I asked.

"No, Matt was the only one there before I left," Valerie said as I took her hand and held it.

Pulling up to the house, Valerie told me there were a lot of cars outside.

"Wow, I didn't expect so many people to be here already," Valerie said, pulling into the driveway. "What's up, Matt?"

"Nothing much," Matt responded.

"Hey, Matt, is Bastian here?" I asked.

"I haven't seen him. You guys want a beer?" Matt asked politely as we walked into the house.

"Please," I said, taking the bottle Matt handed me. "Thank you."

"We needed to talk, remember?" Valerie said, inviting me upstairs.

"Your parents are very proud of you," I said as we walked upstairs. "You have many loving memories in this house."

"How can you tell?" Valerie asked, still holding my hand.

"It's in the air. I can sense it," I said and smiled.

"This is my room," Valerie said as we walked in her room, and she locked the door behind us. "Lord, your scent is intoxicating," Valerie said, smelling my hair as she slowly kissed my neck after she walked up behind me.

"I love you, Danika," Valerie said, biting her lower lip and breathing heavily.

"I love you, Valerie," I said back to her as I smiled.

Valerie

I put my hands on Danika's petite waist. We softly breathed into each other before our soft, moist lips met again. From that very moment on, I knew I never wanted to kiss anyone but her again.

"What are you two doing in there?" Bastian said as he knocked on the door, and we chuckled.

"We were just talking," I said, opening the door, holding Danika's hand.

The rest of the night went by fast. Danika and I were inseparable. Bastian looked like he had a blast as he got a few numbers from some girls.

"Well, I better be on my way," Bastian said as the song "How do I live" played in the background. "Valerie, great party."

"Have a great night, Bastian," Danika said, giving Bastian a hug.

"Well, that's everyone," I said, taking a deep breath before closing the door behind Bastian. "Now where were we?" I asked Danika, putting my hands back on her perfect, trim waist before kissing the soft skin of her neck, working my way up to her lips.

Danika

When morning came, I awoke thinking that last night had just been a beautiful dream. But it wasn't. Reaching under the sheets, I discovered that I was naked. Reaching over to the left side of myself, I felt Valerie's nude body. Saying nothing, I turned so I could run my hands all over her beautiful body.

"You have such beautiful skin," I said, beginning to caress her body all over.

Sitting up, Valerie shifted her body to where she was able to sit on her knees in between my legs. Leaning over, she began french-kissing me. As our tongues met one another, we both gasped. She slowly made her way down to my soft breasts, taking my right nipple into her mouth. She massaged it with her tongue and lips till I took a deep breath. We made love, finding ecstasy when we both climaxed together. We fell back to sleep when we finished.

When I woke up, I quietly found my way to the bathroom.

Turning on the shower, I waited till the temperature was right to get in. As I was slowly getting into the shower, I heard the bed creak as if Valerie was getting up.

"Danika," Valerie said, waking up and seeing I wasn't in bed with her. "Ah, she's in the shower," Valerie said to herself and smiled as she rubbed her eyes.

Raising her nude body gracefully up from the bed, Valerie stretched before walking into the bathroom where I was showering. Standing in the doorway, Valerie stood and watched the water drip off my beautiful petite body. Getting into the shower to join me, she put her arms around me from behind and hugged me.

"Good morning," I said lovingly, putting my hands on hers.

"Good morning back," Valerie said as I turned around to face her, and we gently began kissing.

"I love you," I said and smiled.

"I love you too," Valerie said, taking my hands and putting them on her face.

"I love your smile," I said, feeling so in love.

"Would you go to prom with me, Danika?" Valerie asked.

"Yes," I said, kissing and hugging her.

She began softly lathering my body with soap till I was covered in suds. We sweetly continued kissing one another till the soap on my body was all over hers, and once the water had washed it all away, Valerie began kissing me all over my stomach and chest.

True Love

Maya asked walking into the kitchen, "Nikki, Danika never came home last night, did she?"

"She spent the night at Valerie's," I responded.

"Valerie's?" Maya said, looking away.

"Yes, Valerie's," I responded, "you know, her girlfriend."

"I can't believe you would let her sleep over there," Maya said disapprovingly.

"Well, I let her, and I would let her again. She's seventeen. I for one am happy for her, and you should be too."

"It's just . . ." Maya said hesitating.

"Just what?" I asked.

"Nothing."

"Maya, why don't we get out of the house and go to the mall today? It might be fun."

"All right," Maya said with a deep sigh.

***

Danika

Getting up out of bed after making love one last time, I slipped my clothes on and lay back down, gently rubbing Valerie's back.

"You gonna sleep all day, beautiful?" I asked, continuing to rub her back.

"If you stayed next to me, I could stay here like this for the rest of my life," Valerie said smiling.

"I was thinking, we could go out and look at prom dresses, maybe even go to the mall," I suggested.

"That sounds awesome," Valerie said, touching the side of my face. "Just let me get up," she said stretching. "I loved watching you sleep last night," Valerie said and smiled.

"Did you? I'm surprised you had energy left to keep your eyes open after all the nocturnal activities we performed."

"I'm surprised too, because you wore me out," Valerie said and smiled.

"What can I say, I aim to please," I said, smiling and kissing her.

"Let's not go anywhere. We can stay in bed all day, watch movies and make love," Valerie said.

"As tempting as that is, you did ask me to prom, and now you and I both need a dress."

"Okay," Valerie said, yawning and getting up.

Arriving at the mall, we held hands and went inside. Little did we know, Nikki and my grandmother just pulled into the parking lot after us.

***

"Hey, isn't that Danika right there walking with Valerie?" Maya asked.

"Looks like it," I said and parked. "Maybe we'll see them inside."

Walking into the mall, we looked around to see if we'd see Danika after we tried calling her and she didn't answer.

"Look, there she is on the upper level," Maya said, looking at them curiously. "Is she holding hands with Valerie?"

"No, she's just holding her arm," I shrugged. "You know, so Danika won't have to use her walking stick."

"Yeah, she's holding her arm all right," Maya said, looking at me angrily after Valerie put her hands on Danika's hips and kissed her.

"They both look happy," I said smiling. "What else matters?"

"How do you think it looks when the daughter of Jensen and Octavia Kane is kissing a girl at the mall?" Maya asked, disappointed and shaking her head.

"I don't think it'll look like anything other than happiness, and that's what matters," I said. "Why don't we go up there and see if they want to go to lunch?"

Going up the escalator to the top floor, we saw that Valerie and Danika were still very close together.

"Hey, Mrs. Kane, how are you?" Valerie said, staying confident and standing at my side when Nikki and my grandma approached us.

"Hey, girls," Nikki said excitedly giving us both hugs.

"What are you guys doing here?" I asked.

"We could ask you the same thing, young lady," Maya said rudely.

"It's a pleasure to see you again, Maya," Valerie said.

"Pleasure indeed, Valerie," Maya replied frustrated.

"Do you girls want to join us for lunch?" Nikki asked.

"We'd love to," Valerie said.

"Excellent! Let's get some lunch," Nikki said, excited again.

"Where should we go?" I asked, joining the conversation and feeling my grandmother's cold stare on me.

"What about Chevy's Mexican restaurant?" Valerie said.

When we got to the restaurant, it was packed. Little did I know, Valerie had called ahead to make a reservation, and the restaurant had no problem accommodating two more in our group. As the waiter walked us to our table, I could sense the parade of questions that were coming from my grandma. I know she saw me and Valerie kissing.

Honesty is the best policy, Danika. Deny nothing, and give it to her straight. You love Valerie, and that's the end of the discussion, Tigist said, sharing to me her words of wisdom.

"So how long has this been going on?" Grandma asked, jumping right into her disapproving thoughts as soon as we sat down.

"Well, let's see here . . . I've been gay for literally my entire life. I've had other girlfriends before, but Valerie seems to be the first that really pisses you off. Why is that?"

"Well...," Maya said up before being interrupted.

"You know something. I don't care. I love Valerie, she loves me, and quite frankly, I'm through pretending I'm not gay, Maya," I said frustrated. "Walking on egg shells around you has become a full time job and quite frankly, I'm sick of it."

"Maya? You mean, I'm not even Grandma anymore?" Maya asked sternly.

"Not if you're going to treat me and my girlfriend like this," I said, standing my ground.

"I'm happy you love whom you love, sweetheart, but this has to end," Maya said. "Neither God nor Jesus would ever approve of this nonsense."

"This conversation is over. Have a nice lunch, Maya," I said, getting up from the table and accidentally spilling a cup of water. "Nikki, I'll see you later," I said, taking Valerie's hand and walking away.

"Would you mind explaining yourself?" Nikki demanded. "In all the years I've known you, I've never seen you speak to her like that."

"I just don't want to see her making the wrong choices," Maya said, taking a deep breath.

"Danika, slow down. We're out of the restaurant," Valerie said.

"I'm sorry, I just can't stand that she doesn't accept me for who I am," I said upset.

"I understand. I haven't even come out to my parents," Valerie said. "I fear they may disown me," Valerie said, "and it's no joke when I say it. I really do feel like that."

As Valerie and I went about our day, we both found prom dresses that were unique and beautiful. It was around ten o'clock at night when we pulled up outside my house, and I passionately kissed Valerie goodbye.

"I love you, Valerie," I said as I smelled her beautiful hair.

"I love you, Danika," Valerie said, hugging me before I got out of the car.

Walking up the path to the front door, I heard the car door open.

"Danika, wait!" I heard Valerie say before turning around. "I forgot to give you something."

"What?" I asked.

"This," Valerie said right before I received the kiss that only true love could deliver. Our lips met, and my eyes fluttered shut. I'd never been kissed so passionately. It was perfect, and when it ended, it ended with no words. For nothing either one of us could say could be as perfect as the true love's kiss we'd just shared.

Walking into the house, I sensed that someone was still awake.

"Hi, Danika," I heard Maya's voice say. "Can I talk to you?"

"I don't know, Maya, can you?" I asked frustrated.

"I didn't mean to come off so abrasive earlier," Maya said.

"Are you aware of how prejudiced you are?" I asked concerned.

"I am not prejudiced," Maya said offended.

"Do you recall what you said to me when I began having these feelings toward a girl named Ruth back in middle school?" I asked.

"Yes," Maya said, closing her eyes and remembering. "I told you and her to walk in the light of God and not stray from the path Jesus set forth for him and his followers. You're living in sin."

"Not a day goes by that I don't recall that conversation. Do you remember what I told you?"

"Yes, you said you'd rebel against anyone who'd tell you whom you can and can't love," Maya said.

"I meant it then as I mean it now when I say I love Valerie more than anything in this world, and I'll be damned if I allow anyone to jeopardize that happiness we feel for one another."

"Then I guess our conversation is over," Maya said.

"I guess it is," I replied, walking upstairs to my room.

"I'll let Nikki know in the morning that I'll be moving out."

"Why are you going to move out?"

"Because I can't witness you walk this sinful path. It breaks my heart."

"It's probably for the best then," I said. "You know I never intended to hurt you, Grandma," I said sadly.

"I know."

Reaper of Fallujah

Jensen

It was early morning. The sand on the beach was damp from rain the night before. Looking out at the ocean, I took my surfboard, jabbed it into the sand, and took a deep breath.

Zipping my wet suit up, I saw the men under my command running past me with their boards, splashing into the water. I'd been in command of the Delta Force team Zero for so many years now that I'd lost track. I had made really good friends here—some fallen, some still living.

"I've seen that look before," a man said, walking up behind me.

"It's called serenity, Sergeant Major," I said and smirked. "And I've told you many times before, you ought to try feeling it sometime."

"You know Khatia Dafie raised the bounty on your head, yet again?"

"Yep," I said, looking down at the sand.

"You've managed to really ruffle their feathers."

"Well . . . you know what they say, you go knocking on the devil's door long enough, he may answer," I said, standing next to the sergeant major and looking out at the ocean.

"We've lived many lives, you and I," the sergeant major said as if he wanted to tell me something.

"We have," I replied. "Let's not stand on ceremony today, Dean. Let's get out there and hit those waves."

"Is that an order, sir?" Dean replied. "I mean, Jensen?"

"Hell yeah, it's an order!" I said as we both took off running into the water.

***

After a long day of surfing, we headed back to Camp Pendleton where we'd been stationed before returning to Fort Bragg. Pulling up to the parking lot gate, I knew my team's time off would be cut short when I saw the lieutenant colonel's Hummer in the parking lot. That could only mean we're going back to Fallujah.

"How were the waves, Master Sergeant?" the gate guard asked as I pulled up.

"It was a great day," I nodded. "How long has the lieutenant colonel been here?"

"He just pulled in about fifteen minutes ago, sir," the guard said. "Master Sergeant, can I ask you a question?"

"What's on your mind, Private?" I asked.

"If it's not too much to ask, can I get your autograph?" he asked me as he handed me a copy of *Embrace the Fate* and then a copy of *Razorblade Kiss*.

"Sure," I said, smiling and taking the CDs from the private. "Do you have a Sharpie?"

"Yes, sir," he said, handing me a black Sharpie.

"She was a beautiful person, sir," the guard said as he saw me take a moment to look at Octavia on the cover of *Razorblade Kiss*.

"She was," I said, signing both CDs and handing them back to him.

"Have a nice night, sir," he said as I slowly pulled away.

"Same to you, Private."

Pulling into the parking lot, I parked my truck, jumped out, and regrouped with my men in the main building.

"Gentlemen, as you had seen when we pulled into the parking lot, the lieutenant colonel is on base. We'll regroup tomorrow at 1400 hours for briefing."

"Master Sergeant, we just started our leave," Dean said.

"I understand, Sergeant Major, but we'll do what's asked of us."

"Sir, may we leave base?" Private Trent asked, raising his hand.

"Yes. But no one will be late tomorrow," I said. "Now get out of here and enjoy yourselves, that's an order."

***

"Master Sergeant!" a grumpy lieutenant colonel shouted through a narrow hallway. "You there, where's the master sergeant?" the colonel shouted at a private that monitored the hallways.

"I haven't seen him, sir," the private nervously replied with a salute.

"At ease, soldier. Saluting me is like painting a target on my chest," the colonel said.

"Who's the dune coon, sir?" the private asked with much prejudice in his voice when he saw an Arab man standing behind the colonel.

"The dune coon, as you so elegantly put it, is Majid El-Khatib," the colonel said frustrated. "Now, have you seen the master sergeant?"

"Yes, sir, Colonel. I might have seen him in the gym, sir."

"Son, either you've seen the master sergeant or you haven't, which is it?" the colonel asked sternly.

"The gym, sir. I've seen him there."

"What's your name, Private?"

"Lee, sir!" he said, still standing at attention.

"Are you part of the master sergeant's team, Private Lee?"

"Yes, sir."

"Well, you're part of a great team, and you're lucky to have them, Private," the colonel said, patting the private on the shoulder. "Now take me to the master sergeant."

"Tell me, is Major Rouge with the master sergeant?" the colonel asked, grilling the young private.

"No, sir. The major left base," the private replied.

"I see," the colonel said, shaking his head while walking into the gym behind the private. "Wow! I can't say I've ever seen you without a shirt, Master Sergeant. What's with all the tattoos?"

"Relics of the past, sir," I responded, saluting the colonel.

"Master Sergeant!" the private said, saluting me.

"Lee, what are you still doing in uniform?"

"Guarding the halls, sir," the private responded.

"Who put you up to that?" I asked.

"The sergeant major, sir."

"Okay, well, no more guarding the halls tonight."

"The major played a trick on me, sir?" the private asked.

"Yes, he did," I said. "Remember, Private, at 1400 tomorrow we regroup."

"Yes, sir," the private said, walking out of the gym.

"How have you been, Master Sergeant?" the colonel asked.

"Sir, may we skip all the pleasantries and just get to the point?"

"You've been responsible for countless missions, Master Sergeant. What if I told you that we have the chance right now to strike while the iron is hot?"

"I'm listening," I said.

"There's a price on your head, Master Sergeant. My people believe you're the reaper that has come to collect their souls, they're running scared," Majid El-Khatib said, speaking up.

"Is that what you think?" I asked, looking at Majid.

"Excuse me, Master Sergeant, this is—" the colonel said before being cut off.

"Majid El-Khatib, son of Abdul El-Khatib, the leader and cofounder of Khatia Dafie. But if memory serves me correctly, Majid," I said, taking a minute thinking, "you're supposed to be dead. You were killed in action during the Syrian civil war while taking part in an Inghimasi-style attack on the Syrian army and Russian forces. Sound about right?"

"You're dead-on accurate," Majid said.

"Do you remember me?" I asked, getting in his face.

"How could I forget?" Majid said, standing tall.

"I don't know what evil brought you back, but don't think I won't put you back in the ground if I feel for one moment that my men may be in danger of you," I said as he stood there and glared at me.

"All right, Master Sergeant," the colonel said, trying to calm the situation. "Majid is here to help us. Now, my plan is to drop your team in Ramadi. There we'll go to the Roz Hotel. The team's cover is going to be a channel 5 news crew. Our story will be simple. We're collecting information on the ongoing war. Majid has agreed to turn you over to Al-Rashid for the bounty on your head of $90,000 alive. Being the son of Abdul El-Khatib, Al-Rashid won't even suspect Majid of working with us. When you're close to Al-Rashid, I think it's pretty self-explanatory what you do next."

"What do you get out of this?" I asked, looking at Majid.

"An end to war and a chance to rebuild my country," Majid said. "First thing I will see too is peace throughout all the Middle East. When peace is restored, I will put all my focus into seeing that the third temple in Jerusalem is built."

"What's the real reason?" I asked.

"Listen to me, Kane. I'm sick of the war. Your leaders have agreed that once we've taken out Al-Rashid, the country would be passed over to me to be set right again. So what I have told you is the truth."

"Colonel, am I hearing this right?" I asked, looking at the colonel for confirmation.

"Yes," the colonel said. "I will also be accompanying your team on this mission. Orders have come from the Pentagon that I'm to assist and observe. After you're taken, your team and I will hold back until the opportunity arises. When that happens, your team and I will infiltrate Al Rashid's hideout and assist you."

"This is the best plan we've got?" I asked, looking at the colonel.

"It's the only plan we have. Trust no one, Master Sergeant," the colonel said.

"Understood, sir. I'll brief the men," I said before looking at Majid. "As for you, I'm willing to die for my country and my men. Can you say the same?" I asked, glaring at Majid. "Know this, if you step out of line, I'll make sure you never do so again."

"Is that a threat?" Majid asked.

"It's a promise," I responded.

"You know, I'm not the threat, nor am I the enemy you make me to be," Majid said.

"We'll see," I said, walking past him and out of the gym.

***

"Private, have you seen the sergeant major?" I asked.

"No, sir, he left the base last night and has not returned," the private said.

"Master Sergeant, I don't want anyone on this mission who can't show up on time," the colonel said firmly.

"Knowing the sergeant major, he probably has a good reason."

"For your sake, I hope he does," Majid said, condescending in Arabic.

"Don't think for a second that I don't understand you," I said, slowly walking over to Majid and shoving him to the floor.

"Master Sergeant, you are out of line," the colonel shouted as Private Trent and one of the other men grabbed me.

"That's all right," Majid said, getting up off the floor. "I know you don't trust me, and that's okay."

"With all due respect, sir, this is a mistake," Private Trent said to the colonel. "Snubbing the sergeant major, you should be ashamed of yourself."

"Private, you better choose your next words very carefully, or you will find yourself cut from the mission alongside the sergeant major."

"Trent, stand down," I said, turning around and looking at him. "Stand down. Collect your thoughts and have a seat," I continued, taking a deep breath. "You know, it's not a good idea to enrage my men," I said, looking at Majid, "especially me. But Trent's right, Colonel, it's not a good idea to snub the sergeant major like this."

"I understand. But my orders remain," the colonel said.

"Yes, sir," I said, pausing for a moment. "Men, have a seat, and I'll brief you on the mission," I said as my team sat in their seats and awaited briefing.

Lessons from Jesus

Danika

That night I slept carefree and without worry. When I awoke the next morning, I could feel the warmth of the sun on my face. I felt rough, dry dirt all around me. Trying to open my eyes, I found they felt weak and heavy. But to my surprise, I saw blurry images everywhere. I continued to look around, squinting until things finally began to come into focus.

"Tigist, where are you?" I said, looking around.

I'm here, Danika, Tigist said as she flew down from a wooden post onto my forearm.

"I can see," I said, looking at Tigist smiling.

Yes, you can, Danika.

Standing up, I saw that I was asleep on the side of a dirt road. I saw a man dressed in a light-colored tunic, walking with people, educating them about God. His voice was soft but direct. He was tall, white, and handsome. His beard was long and groomed. His hair was long and tied into a ponytail.

"Tigist," he called out as I saw an owl fly to him and land on his forearm. He looked at a very attractive woman on the side of the road.

"Jesus, did this woman sin?" one of the men around him asked as he noticed she was blind.

"Haven't we all, Peter?" Jesus said. "None of us are without sin."

"My Lord, she is a harlot," Judas said as Jesus kindly walked over to the woman and placed his hand on her shoulder.

"It's you," the blind girl said as soon as Jesus touched her shoulder.

"And who am I, child?" Jesus asked.

"The Son of Man," she said, "our Lord and Savior, Jesus Christ."

"I am," Jesus said as he took her hands in his.

"Evil is within me, Lord. I am not worthy of your forgiveness," she said weeping.

"What is your name?" Jesus asked.

"Mary," she replied.

"Mary, there is no evil within you. Everyone is worthy of forgiveness if they seek it. I am the light, and I will work the blessings of my Father as I see fit," Jesus said as he wetted the tips of both his thumbs with his saliva. "Close your eyes, child."

I watched as he carefully rubbed a little dirt on both his thumbs. He gently wiped the dirt on Mary's eyelids.

"Mary, would you care to walk with me?" Jesus asked politely as he helped her to her feet with the dirt still on her eyes as all those with him looked on.

"I'd love to," she said, interlocking her arm with his. "Where are you taking me?"

"To one of the pools of Solomon. When we're there, you will wash your face and look upon your reflection for the first time. You will then see that I, the Son of Man, can work the wonders of my Father," Jesus said, helping Mary into Solomon's pool to do what he asked of her.

Once there she washed her face as directed by Jesus. Opening her eyes for the first time, the darkness faded away. Looking at the palms of her hands, she turned them every which way. Then she saw her reflection in the water and began to cry. Walking out from the water, she looked around to see where Jesus was, but he was nowhere to be seen.

As she walked the streets of Jerusalem, people began asking Mary how she came to have sight. This soon caught the interest of Joseph Caiaphas, a high priest and an ally to Rome.

Mary soon found herself brought before him.

"How is it that you are able to see?" Joseph Caiaphas asked. "We all know very well who you are, Mary Magdalene, the blind whore."

"The Son of Man stood before me. He made a sort of clay and anointed my eyes. He then had me wash the clay off in the pool of Solomon. When this was done, I was able to see," Mary explained.

"You know it's forbidden to enter the pools of Solomon?" Caiaphas asked her.

"I did not know," Mary said.

"You must understand, Jesus is not a man of God," Caiaphas said sternly.

"Then how does he perform such miracles?" Mary asked.

"My child, a man of God observes the Sabbath day," another priest said, looking at Mary. "He has indeed been touched to perform such miracles, but not by God."

"Then by what?" Mary asked confused.

"Not by what, but by whom, my dear," Caiaphas said.

"That is blasphemy," Mary said aloud.

"What did you say?" a different priest sneered.

"How do you not see? He is the Word of God," Mary said. "He is the Son of Man."

"We are Moses's disciples. We know that God spoke to Moses. We do not know what depths of darkness Jesus came from. Now leave my sight, and don't let me hear of you associating with Jesus or his followers again," Caiaphas said. "And do not speak of this to anyone."

Mary was escorted out of the temple. When she walked out into the streets, she saw Jesus waiting for her.

"Do you believe that I'm the Son of God?" Jesus asked.

"I do," she said, falling into Jesus's arms, hugging him. "I betrayed you, my Lord. I told Caiaphas that you healed me. Forgive me," Mary said, beginning to cry.

"Do not cry. There is nothing to forgive," Jesus said.

Just then I accidentally made a noise from the shadows.

"Who might you be, little one?" Jesus said, looking into the darkness.

"Jesus, who are you talking to?" Mary asked.

"The young girl that hides in the shadows," he said. "Will you not come out and introduce yourself?"

"I'm Danika, my Lord," I said, walking out from the shadows.

"You don't need to explain anything. I know why you've

come. Would you care to join Mary and I for supper, Danika?" Jesus asked.

"I'd love to," I replied.

***

The next morning I woke up, and I knew immediately I was still with Jesus, judging by the blanket that was on the hard dirt ground. Getting up, I walked around his home that was made of solid rock and looked around.

"Good morning, Danika," Jesus said as he stretched.

"Good morning," I replied.

"Would you like to join me for breakfast?" he asked.

"Sure."

Sitting down at a wooden table, I saw dry figs and grapes, pomegranate juice, milk, and some yogurt.

"Wow, things are very different where I'm from," I said, picking up one of the figs.

"How so?" Jesus asked.

"We have bacon, eggs, sausage. Hash browns are my favorite," I said excitedly. "Oh, Jesus, you would love it."

"What's a hash brown?" Jesus asked curiously.

"They're amazing. They're thinly shredded potatoes you cook in a skillet, with a little oil and salt, and brown them."

"Well, they sound delightful, Danika," Jesus said and smiled. "So . . . I've been meaning to ask, what's with the clothes?" Jesus asked.

"What do you mean?" I asked.

"Does everyone in the future dress . . . so odd?"

"I think what you're wearing is odd. Are you even wearing underwear underneath that tunic?"

"What's underwear?" Jesus asked as I smiled and laughed. "What's so funny?" He smiled and chuckled. "And this shirt you're wearing—Embrace the Fate, what is that?"

"So this is my parents' band, they sing music," I said explaining.

"I love music," Jesus said.

"The music in my time is probably way more aggressive than what you're used to here," I said.

"How so?" Jesus asked. "When you say aggressive, do you mean violent?" Jesus asked. "I detest violence."

"No, it's aggressive in a good way."

"Sounds confusing," Jesus said.

"Well, if you heard my parents' band, you'd love it."

"I'm sure I would," Jesus said. "Can you sing for me?" Jesus asked politely.

"I'd love to, but I don't have any instruments," I said.

"Could you use a harp to play?" Jesus asked.

"Well, maybe," I said, thinking of it while accepting the harp Jesus gave me.

Slowly I began to strum the harp and tried to find a tune that would fit. Then I began to sing softly.

***

(Danika sings in soft melody.)
Lie awake
Watching you sleep and dream
I pull you close and breathe you in deep
Your smile stretches from cheek to cheek
Your face is so perfect and sweet
The love we share is so true and deep
Together as one, apart as two
Our love has to be true

The love we share
Forever and true
Whatever the endeavor
Together we'll see it through
We are together forever in a love that's true
So please let's make our love true

I've been awake
Lying here watching you watch me
I pull you close and breathe you in deep
In your dreams, those loving dreams
So real and true
Is where I'll lie and wait for you

You loving me and me loving you
It's true love as our dreams come true
Apart as two
Until you found me and I found you
Together forever, our love is real
Our love is true

(Danika and Jesus sing together in soft melody.)
The love we share
Forever and true
Whatever the endeavor
Together we'll see it through
We are together forever in a love that's true
Now I know our love is true

(Song fades.)

***

"That was beautiful. Absolutely beautiful!" Jesus said, very happy and excited.

"I'm so glad you enjoyed it," I said and smiled. "I wrote that. One day when I regroup Embrace the Fate, it will be number 1 on the charts. I guarantee it."

"Say, would you like to go into town with me today?" Jesus asked. "There are people who sing in the marketplace."

When we left to go into town, we were slowly met on the streets by all of Jesus's disciples. I loved listening to him speak about God. He was very knowledgeable, and much of what he said were things I already knew from Tigist's teachings. But his voice was soothing to hear, and he never raised it. He was always calm and collected. While we all sat in a circle listening to him, we saw Mary thrown to the ground by a group of men that were calling her cruel names and berating her.

"Why do you say such things to my friend?" Jesus asked, standing up and walking up to the men.

"My Lord, Moses spoke of selling your flesh and said that any woman who commits this sin shall be cast out and stoned," a rugged man said, looking at Jesus.

Saying nothing, Jesus knelt down, making eye contact with Mary. He looked her in the eyes, smiled, and helped her to her feet.

"My Lord, what hath you say?" the rugged man asked.

"I say, the first person to cast a stone will be the first person to die on this day," Jesus said calmly. "I have forgiven her sins, and therefore she has been cleansed of all past transgressions. Unless there's another reason you treat her this way."

"By what authority can you grant forgiveness, Jesus?" Joseph Caiphias asked, walking up from out of nowhere.

"And there's the other reason I spoke of," Jesus said and smirked. "Before I answer your question, I have one of my own. Was John the Baptist baptized by heaven or by men?"

"We cannot tell you this," Caiphias said.

"Then I in turn cannot tell you by what authority I do these things," Jesus said, walking over to us and looking at Judas oddly, as if he knew something.

***

That night I attended the private wedding ceremony where Jesus and Mary were joined in holy matrimony. Their union was something of pure beauty, and I felt blessed in having been witness to it.

"I know of the shame you carry, Danika, and you should not feel ashamed. For God made you the way you are, and you are perfect," Jesus said, walking up to me as I looked out at the Jordan River.

"Then you know?" I asked.

"I do," Jesus said.

"How did you discover this?" I asked.

"There is love in your aura. I can see that love is for a very special girl. That song you sang, you were very passionate when you sang it, it revealed your heart. I saw someone very special to you through your thoughts, someone named Valerie. Do not feel ashamed. Be who you are, and love who you are," Jesus said.

"But, my Lord, wasn't it you who said, '*If a man lies with another man as with a woman, both of them have committed an abomination, they must be put to death*'? And Paul said, '*Do not be deceived, neither the sexually immoral, nor idolaters, nor adulterers, nor men who practice homosexuality . . . will inherit the kingdom of God.'"*

"You read the Bible?" Jesus asked.

"I did, and some of what you said has been heartbreaking."

"I understand, but I am human and make mistakes. Maybe it was you, Danika, that has come to teach me. Can you forgive me?" Jesus asked.

"Always," Danika said, giving Jesus a hug. "Your wedding is beautiful, and I'm glad I got to see it."

"I've watched you, Danika. Your eyes are filled with joy and amazement at the sight of things. We're all born without sight but not without purpose. You have spent years without it, but here I say, without sight you will remain till the time comes for you to see again. There is no trick I can teach you to undo your blindness," Jesus said. "But what I can tell you is this, on the day the Nexus appears to you, that will be the day you will no longer be without sight."

"What's the Nexus?" I asked.

"You'll know it when it happens," Jesus said and smiled. "Come, Danika, let us get back to the celebration."

That night after Jesus's wedding, I went to bed. The following morning, I woke up in my room. Sitting up, I opened my eyes, and I was in darkness once more as Jesus said I'd be.

Going Rouge

Jensen

Mohammed Al-Rashid—first general emir and founder of Khatia Dafie. To think I could end this reign of terror with just one stroke of the Nevillin. It all sounded too easy, and what angle was Majid playing? Why was he working with us so willingly? This was the question I needed the answer to the most. Then scrubbing Dean from the mission altogether. Why did the colonel do this?

"Jensen, I just saw Trent. He told me something I don't believe," Dean said, looking angry while walking up to me in the cafeteria. "Is it true?"

"Dean, have a seat," I said calmly.

"No!" Dean shouted, hitting the table with his fist. "Look me in the eye, and tell me you didn't go along with this."

"Dean, sit now! That's an order!" I demanded.

"All right," Dean said, sitting down frustrated, "I'm sitting."

"These orders were passed down from above. But I have no intention of seeing them followed. There's something that's bothering me about the colonel, but I don't know what it is yet. Normally he would have never ordered your removal from the mission."

"You've got my attention," Dean said. "What's your plan?"

"I've already set everything up for you. You are to go to the High Crest Hotel in Ramadi, it's three blocks away from the team at the Roz Hotel. Your cover is that you're a journalist in town writing a piece on the general misunderstandings of the war in Ramadi. The first night you're there, you will have a visit from

Amir Bagnad. He'll see that you receive the care package I send you."

"Ruben Foss?" Dean said, looking inside a manila envelope that I handed him and seeing IDs and passports with his picture on it. "I don't look like a Ruben."

"It's the best I could come up with in such a short time," I said as Dean flipped through the fake credit cards and passports.

"How do you know we can trust Amir, especially after what he did the last time we encountered him?"

"I don't, but I trust you can handle it," I said.

"That I can do," Dean said, reassuring me.

"You have your orders, Major. Your flight leaves tomorrow morning," I said, handing Dean his flight itinerary.

***

Dean

It was 5:00 a.m. and overcast. I took an Uber from Camp Pendleton to John Wayne Airport. When I arrived it was quiet, and I could smell coffee in the air from a Coffee Bean and Tea Leaf nearby. My mission and coordinates were clear. Yet I couldn't stop thinking about what the colonel's plans could be for Jensen if he is corrupted.

"Excuse me, sir. But do I know you from somewhere?" a young Hawaiian boy around the age of eleven asked.

"Where do you think you know me from?" I asked as his mom looked at me and smiled.

"You're Dean Rouge," the kid said firmly.

"How can you be so sure?" I smiled.

"You're only the best drummer in the world, according to *Metal Reigns* magazine," the kid said, pulling out the magazine with me on the cover holding drumsticks.

"Wow, I haven't seen this in years," I said, taking the magazine and looking at it.

"Could you sign it?" the kid asked politely.

"No problem," I said.

"Mom, do you have a pen?" the boy asked.

"I do," Ally said, reaching into her purse and handing me a

black Sharpie.

"When I grow up, I want to be just like you," the kid said smiling.

"Are you a drummer?" I asked and smirked.

"Yes. One day I'll be the greatest," the boy said. "Whom did you look up to?"

"Jimmy Sullivan," I said before going through the metal detector.

"The Rev!" the boy shouted excitedly as I smirked.

"You know your drummers, kid. No one's better than the Rev," I said, giving the boy a fist bump.

"I still think you're the greatest, Dean!" the boy said.

"What's your name?" I asked politely.

"My name's Kai," the boy said, introducing himself.

"Pleasure to meet you, Kai," I said, shaking his hand. "And you are?" I asked, looking at the girl Kai called mom.

"Allison," she said, shaking my hand. "But you can call me Ally."

"It's a pleasure to meet you both," I said before walking in the opposite direction.

After waiting a couple of hours to board the plane, they finally opened the terminal for everyone to board. When I got on the plane and saw my seat, it had the number 57 stitched into the leather.

"Hello," Ally said, walking up behind me.

"Well, hello again," I said back.

"Dean," Kai said excitedly.

"I see your seat 57," Ally said. "Looks like we'll be sitting together. I'm seat 58."

"Excellent," I said, getting up. "Let me help you put your stuff in the overhead storage," I said, taking her carry-on bag and placing it in the overhead storage.

"So, Dean," Ally said, "I feel like I know you," looking at me as I sat down next to her. "And I know you're a famous drummer. But that's not it, you have such familiar eyes."

"I just have one of those faces, I guess," I said.

"I guess so," Ally said thinking. "Why are you going to Ramadi?"

"Business," I said and smiled.

"What kind of business do you do?" Ally asked.

"The kind no one talks about," I said.

"The Rouge kind?" Kai said and smiled.

"That's funny, but right," I said. "I'm going 'rouge,'" I said.

"It almost sounds like the title of a book or a movie," Kai said.

"Sir, I think your son needs help with his belt, we're about to take off," a stewardess said, pointing to Kai's seat belt.

"Oh, he's not my son," I said, helping Kai.

"Oh, I apologize. The three of you just looked so happy, I assumed you were all together."

"Thank you," Ally said and smiled.

"Did you hear that, Mom? She thought Dean was my dad," Kai said excitedly.

"I heard."

"So where are you guys on your way to?" I asked.

"Hawaii, to visit family," Ally answered.

"You okay, Kai?" I asked concerned as we took off and he looked petrified.

"He's afraid of flying," Ally said. "Once we're in the air, he'll be fine. It's always the initial takeoff that really gets to him."

"You want to hold my hand, buddy?" I asked as he latched on to my arm.

After about an hour or so into the flight, I found myself falling in love with Ally. When we smiled at one another, I knew wherever this girl was, I wanted to be there too.

"What?" Ally asked as we looked at one another. "So what should we talk about now?" she said, looking over at Kai, seeing that he'd fallen asleep. "I've seen you glance at my finger twice during this flight, Dean," Ally said.

"Was I being that obvious?" I asked.

"The answer to your question is, no, I'm not married," Ally said and smiled. "I had Kai when I was very young. I made some dumb choices, but I wouldn't change them for anything," Ally said, looking at Kai.

"What's your last name?" I asked.

"Hart."

***

When we landed in Hawaii International Airport, the second I walked off the plane I smelled coffee again. Looking around, I saw another Coffee Bean and Tea Leaf.

"Airports must love Coffee Bean and Tea Leaf," I said. "Ally, I have a three-hour layover. Would you and Kai care to join me for a late lunch, early dinner?"

"That would be lovely," Ally said as she and Kai grabbed their duffel bags off a conveyor belt at baggage.

After eating at Ruby's Diner inside the airport, we were approached by a Hawaiian man wearing a lei.

"Hey you," he said, coming up behind Kai.

"Keleva," Ally said, standing up and giving the man a big hug. "Dean, I want you to meet my older brother, Keleva."

"Dean Rouge," Keleva said. "Embrace the Fate is one of my all-time favorite bands."

"Thanks, man," I said, sad to see Ally go.

"Well, I guess this is where we part ways," Ally said and smiled. "Let me see your phone, Dean," Ally said as I handed her my phone. "You know, for two people who just met, you and I sure do have a lot of chemistry," she said, taking my hands.

"I wouldn't mind staying here," I said before kissing her.

"Then stay," Ally said, smiling.

"Unfortunately, I can't," I said as we smiled at each other one last time.

"Dean, are we going to see you again?" Kai asked.

"For sure, buddy," I said, smiling at Kai. "I'll miss you, guys," I said, kissing Ally one last time.

Walking back to the terminal, I waited for the plane to board before I was approached by two men.

"Mr. Rouge?" one of them asked.

"I was wondering when you guys were going to make your move," I said and chuckled. "You guys should be ashamed of yourselves. You're both very conspicuous. What Mickey Mouse agency do you work for?"

"We work for Rashad Natas," one of them said.

Getting up slowly, I suddenly stretched as if I were going to hit them.

"Ah! I gotcha. You guys thought I was going to hit you."

"For a minute there . . . ," one of them was saying before I pushed them both to the floor and ran.

Running out of the terminal, I went back to where the Coffee Bean and Tea Leaf was, around a bunch of small stores. While I hid in a toy store, I watched as the two men ran past me. Grabbing a sack of marbles, I came out of the store.

"Hey, guys!" I shouted at them as they turned around. "Over here!"

When they began to run at me, I ran the other way, breaking open the sack of marbles all over the floor. I watched as they fell to the ground. Smiling still, I kept running till I was in a parking lot. Looking around and seeing no one, I took out my phone to call Jensen when I was struck over the head. Falling to the ground, I looked up to see a bald, very masculine black man towering over me.

"Dean Rouge, I've waited a long time to make your acquaintance," he said in a deep Russian accent. "I'm Rashad Natas."

Hollow Threats

Shaking his head discouraged as we walked into class, Bastian said, "I hate math class."

"It's not that bad," I said, playing with my Dutch French braid.

"That's easy for you to say, Danika. You're a soon to be valedictorian."

"Am I now?" I laughed.

"Sure, you excel in everything," Bastian said. "You're a blind girl that knows how to surf. Explain that."

"How's it going there, pool cue?" Justin said, coming up behind me.

"Why don't you shut up, Justin!" Bastian said.

"What? The little dyke can't defend herself?" Justin said.

"Are you looking to get your jaw broken?" Bastian said, threatening Justin.

"Anytime, anyplace," Justin replied.

"Okay, okay! Listen, I'm flattered you'd dump Ashley for me, Justin, but you know . . . you're really not my type," I said as all the students in class looked on in shock. "Imagine the rumors that are going to start now, Justin."

"Justin, Danika, Bastian, in your seats! Now!" Mr. Woodsy shouted. "That goes for everyone. Get in your seats."

After sitting down, I could sense Justin glaring at me.

"So what's your problem anyway?" I asked him.

"You insulted Ashley the other day," he said.

"You shouldn't believe everything she tells you," I said.

"Are you calling her a liar?" Justin asked.

"If the shoe fits," I replied, shaking my head.

"Justin, come solve the problem I've put on the board please," Mr. Woodsy said.

When Justin got up from his seat, he tried to push me while I was sitting at my desk. Smoothly and without problem, I moved out of the way, causing him to trip over the leg of my desk.

"What the hell, freak!" Justin shouted angrily after he hit the floor.

"Did you see that?" a student said aloud.

"That was funny," a different student responded laughing.

"Danika!" Mr. Woodsy shouted as I got up from my seat.

"That was awesome," Bastian said, shocked and laughing. "How did you do that?"

"Get back in your seat, Danika," Mr. Woodsy said, walking over.

"Perhaps you should be more careful next time, Justin," I said, smirking and sitting back down.

"Justin, get up and sit at your desk," Mr. Woodsy said.

After taking my seat, it wasn't long till I was sent to the principal's office. Once there I sat and waited to be called into Mr. Reed's office.

"Danika, have a seat," he said politely, inviting me into his office. "Tell me what happened."

After telling him what occurred between Justin and I, he walked out of the office. When he returned, he had two pieces of paper.

"What are the papers for?" I asked.

Taking a moment, he waved his hand in front of my face.

"Mr. Reed, I may be blind, but I haven't lost the use of my other senses," I said, making it a point for him to know that I was no one to underestimate.

"How do you do that?" he asked.

"What?"

"See without seeing. How did you know I had two pieces of paper?"

"I heard two pieces of paper crinkle, and they both have fresh ink on them. I know this because I can smell the ink," I said frustrated. "Just as I can tell you with the utmost certainty that you have been wearing the same shirt and tie for the last couple of days, a shirt that has been sprayed with a cheap Tommy Hilfiger cologne and not cleaned properly. I can smell the fresh cologne mixed with the old cologne, and your body odor is rancid," I said. "Now, as I asked already, what are the two papers for?"

"One is a detention form for Justin, and the other is an assault form for you to fill out since Justin put his hands on you."

"This is a very backward system," I said thinking.

"Excuse me?" Mr. Reed said irritated.

"First of all, he didn't hurt me. Second thing is, he tried to put his hands on me and failed," I said. "So there was no assault."

"But, Danika, we don't care about that. What we care about is that he tried to hurt you, and what makes it worse is that you have a disability."

"Ah, now the truth comes out," I replied. "So how do I get put in detention?" I asked, unfolding my cane.

"I'm sorry?" Mr. Reed asked.

"You heard me," I said, taking my cane and sliding everything off the principal's desk. "Now what are you going to do?" I asked him.

"Okay, Ms. Kane, here's your detention form," Mr. Reed said as he handed me the assault form and the detention form.

"You know, Mr. Reed, you shouldn't pity those who you think may be weak," I said, crumpling up the assault form. "They're much stronger than you think."

"You know, I've been dealing with your family for years, Danika. Jensen, Octavia, Connor—all valedictorians. Except for Jensen, for all the obvious reasons. But nonetheless, your dad was a bright student. Hopefully, you don't go the same road as he did," Mr. Reed said. "I'm tired of your family. So just think of your time in detention as you serving your parents' time and your own. I don't know how, but they always evaded detention and got away with it."

"As will I," I responded.

"Not as far as I'm concerned. You, like your parents, are to be a valedictorian. But don't think for one second I can't put an end to that."

"I totally understand, Mr. Reed," I said, standing up and putting my hand on his. "I will be a valedictorian. If you think for one second I'll allow you to jeopardize that, you're dreadfully mistaken. There will be no detention for Justin or I, and you will brush this under the carpet. You'll forget this conversation even took place," I said, removing my hand from his.

"Can I help you, Danika?" Mr. Reed asked, shaking his head as if he had just woken up from a dream.

"I was sent up to your office by Mr. Woodsy," I said.

"Go back to class, Danika," he said, walking me out of his office. "Justin, what are you doing up here?"

"I was sent up here by Mr. Woodsy," Justin said confused.

"You may go back to class," Mr. Reed said.

"What did you say to him?" Justin whispered, walking up beside me.

"I got us both out of serving detention," I said.

"How did you do that?" Justin asked.

"I have my ways," I said.

"So what now?" Justin asked.

"What do you mean?" I asked.

"Well, I kinda owe you for doing this," Justin said.

"We're going back to the way things have always been."

"And how was that?"

"You know, you and your friends teasing and picking on everybody here at school," I said.

"No, not anymore," Justin said, giving me a small but meaningful hug.

"That'd be nice," I replied.

"Cool," Justin said as we walked back into class.

After getting back to class, the rest of the day became a blur. The last period of my day was the hardest as I wanted to go home and tell Nikki what I did to Mr. Reed. When the bell finally rang, I grabbed my stuff and bolted out the door to meet Bastian by the bike rack so we could get on the public bus together, but he never showed up. Getting on the bus, I noticed immediately that it was a different driver from the one a couple of weeks ago. That was when my nose caught the scent of Pink Friday, a perfume from Nicki Minaj.

"Pink Friday," I whispered, focusing on the smell.

"Dang, girl," the bus driver said happy and excitedly, "you caught my scent."

"Well, of course. Pink Friday is only the greatest perfume

out right now," I smiled as I was a big fan of Niki Minaj.

"Any fan of Nicki Minaj is a friend of mine," the driver said happily. "What's your name, sweetheart?"

"Danika Kane. Pleasure to meet you."

"A very pretty name for such a pretty girl, Danika, and I love your hair. Is that a Dutch French braid?"

"Yes. It's my favorite hairstyle."

"Well, listen, Danika, anything you need, I got you. My name is Chantel."

"Let's go, pool cue," Ashley said from behind me.

"Get a move on," another girl rudely said.

"Oh, no way! You're gonna be talking to my girl like that," Chantel said with an attitude.

"Well, she won't move," Ashley said annoyed.

"And for good reason. I'm talking to her," Chantel said. "All right, Danika, go have a seat, baby."

"It's about time," Ashley whispered.

"Excuse you, young lady, you and your friends will have to wait for the next bus or find other means of transportation today," Chantel said firmly.

"OMG! Are you serious?" Ashley said before looking at her friends.

"As a heart attack," Chantel said. "And don't you girls speak English anymore? What's *OMG*?" Chantel asked, rolling her eyes and closing the door of the bus on the girls as they stood outside.

"Where's Justin?" I heard Ashley say as she hung up her smartphone, looking at her friends.

When we got to my stop, I got off the bus and began walking home when I heard someone cry out for help from the woods nearby. Focusing on the noises around me, I began to walk in the direction of where I heard the cry for help.

Danika, where are we going? Tigist asked as I flicked my wrist and she appeared.

"Someone's in trouble, Tigist," I said.

We don't know that for sure, Danika, Tigist said, flying in front of me. *I'll scout up ahead and see what's out there.*

Now you're talking, I said as Tigist flew ahead.

Through Tigist's eyes I saw Justin tied up. There were trees, and he was sitting with his back to a rock. He was bleeding from his forehead. It was the bus driver that Bastian and I met from the morning route.

"God's avenging angel is coming for you. / Daughter of man, I'm out to get you. / Evil, lock your doors. / Quickly run and hide, I'm coming for you," I sang, walking through the woods with my cane out.

"What is that?" the bus driver said, hearing my voice singing nearby.

"Danika, get out of here!" Justin shouted.

"So what song were you singing," the bus driver asked as I could see through Tigist's eyes that he came up from behind me and put a knife to my throat, "my darling?"

"That was 'Embrace the Fate,'" I said calmly.

"That'll be the last song you ever sing or hear, my dear," he said, tightening his grasp. "Now shut up," he said, cutting my arm a bit.

"Where's the cut on your arm?" he asked as it slowly vanished, and he slowly let me go.

"You should ask for forgiveness," I said.

"Danika, move!" Justin shouted, running up behind the bus driver and clobbering him in the back of the head with a thick tree branch.

"Ahhh!" the man grunted after falling to the ground.

"Justin, no more," I said, putting my hand on his chest to stop him. "He's finished."

"Finished?" Justin shouted angrily. "He's a murderer, Danika!" Justin shouted in anger.

"I know," I said, turning and looking at the man.

"What do you mean you know?" Justin asked confused.

"Justin, take a deep breath," I said as he calmed down. "Tigist," I said, and she came flying down from a tree onto my forearm.

"What is your name?" I asked the man.

"Will," he said frightened, looking at me.

"William, look at me," I said, gently lifting his face upward. "I want you to go to the police station and turn yourself in. You'll go to prison. But while you're there, you will devote your life to me and spread the Word of Christ to all who'll listen. Do this, and I will remember you on judgment day."

"Who are you?" he asked as I just smiled but didn't answer.

Justin

I watched Danika mesmerized. I'd never seen anything like it before. I listened as the man confessed all his sins to her as if she could forgive him of his transgressions.

"Please forgive me," Will begged as he began to weep.

"Will, I want you to go now and remember your oath," Danika said as Will got up from the ground.

"I will walk the line as you did, my Lord," Will said, bowing his head and walking away.

"What the hell did I just witness?" I asked.

"A miracle," Danika said.

"How were you able to do that?" I asked. "Are you a witch?"

"No," Danika said and chuckled. "I'm something else entirely."

Finding Spraygin

Danika

The next morning when I awoke, there was a cold, eerie smell of death in the air. My eyes burned. Rubbing them, I began to adjust to the darkness, and I could see again. My vision was blurred, but as I looked around, I saw that the walls around me were plain and boring. A single coat of paint was all that stained the wall. On the door was a small opening with metal bars.

Danika, are you okay? Tigist asked as I periodically rubbed my eyes.

"Tigist, everything is really blurry," I said squinting, "and my eyes burn."

I think we time-jumped again, Tigist said, flying around.

"Really, Colombo?" I said sarcastically, looking around.

Funny, Tigist said unamused.

"EJDC," I read aloud while looking at the bed frame in the room. "What's EJDC?"

Eastlake Juvenile Detention Center, Tigist said thinking.

"That would mean . . ." I said thinking.

Your father is here, Tigist said. *You know, if you meet him, he can't know who you are,* Tigist said firmly.

"Don't worry, Tigist. I'm a really good actress," I said with an assured smile.

Walking up to the door, I checked it to see if it would open. Turning the handle, I opened the door and looked down a dark hallway, still rubbing my eyes to get them to focus. I stepped out and walked down the dark hallway when I came up to another door. Opening it, I saw showers.

Quick, hide! Someone's coming, Tigist said, flying high up to one of the exposed rusty water pipes above.

I heard talking close by, then all of a sudden a door entering the showers opened. Hiding behind a wall, I watched two guards take a young boy, around seventeen, in handcuffs and hang him from the exposed rusty water pipes in the ceiling. Walking into the showers shortly after the guards, a middle-aged woman walked up to the boy and began seducing him and asking him if he enjoyed pain. Then she slowly touched his upper body.

The boy had no fear in his eyes as he looked her in the eyes and told her, "Do what you need to do."

A doctor in the room drew blood from his arm and began speaking about angel blood and its health benefits and healing factors.

Cutting her own hand, the woman took the boy's blood and put it in the cut on her hand. Before my eyes, I watched as her hand healed immediately.

"How do you know of this, you're human?" the boy asked.

"Let's just say, I have my connections," she answered.

"You'll never get away with this," the boy said.

"Ah, but that's where you're wrong," the woman said.

"Well, you just got the perfect operation going on here, don't you?" the boy said.

"Don't patronize me, Mr. Kane. We're both killers in our own rights," the woman said as the doctor finished taking his blood and left the room.

"Mr. Kane?" I whispered. "Dad."

"Did you hear something?" one the guards asked, looking at the other.

The guards slowly walked over to the wall I was hiding behind. I flew up like lightning to the pipes in the ceiling and disappeared into the darkness and perched myself on a rusty old pipe. After finding nothing, they took my father and left. I made my way back out to the hallway. Once there, a guard came up behind me with a gun. Instead of fighting, I did what I was told. He escorted me to a dark room where he left me. After a few minutes, he returned with another guard.

"Frank, I'll keep a lookout and make sure no one disturbs you," one guard told the other.

"Jerry, this is the last time, right?" Frank asked.

"She must be the last one. I already got rid of the others," Jerry answered.

"Time for you and I to get acquainted, sweetheart," Frank said, looking at me and taking off his utility belt.

"You've gotta be kidding me," I said, rolling my eyes.

"Come on, little darlin', this could be pleasurable for you too," he said as he reached out to touch me. "And you won't remember anything, I promise. Indulge."

"Perhaps you're right," I said, grabbing his hand and breaking it. "I bet that hurt, didn't it?" I said as the other guard, Jerry, walked in and locked the door behind him.

"This is quite the operation you have going on here, isn't it?" I said. "Sex trafficking, really?"

"It was quite lucrative till Mr. Natas gave the order to have it taken down. No more sex trafficking, no more organ harvesting. To think we were so close to finally procuring the organ he needed from that boy."

"Procuring the organ from a certain someone?" I asked curiously.

"Yeah, some jinn boy that's always hanging around with Jensen Kane."

"Dean," I said softly.

"That's the one, Dean Rouge," Jerry said excited. "Wait a second . . . how do you know that name?"

"We knew you'd come," Frank said, getting up from the ground and swiping his good hand over the broken one.

"Frank, you know this girl?" Jerry asked, scared as Frank showed me his hand was no longer broken.

"All too well, my friend," Frank said, flicking his wrist, and a bloodied cleaver appeared.

Danika, flick your wrist, Tigist said immediately after Frank stabbed Jerry in the stomach.

"Frank," Jerry said shocked, before falling to the floor.

"No hard feelings, buddy," Frank said, ripping the cleaver out of him.

When I flicked my wrist, the Nexus appeared. As I took a

moment to look at it, I saw it had a blue sparkle to it. I could sense a certain positive aura surrounding it. Frank then came running at me full speed. Stepping to the side, I took the Nexus and sliced him in half at the belly. As he slowly disappeared into a dark smoke, I looked at the Nexus and smiled, and again a sparkle came down the blade as it did before.

"Jesus' spirit resides within the Nexus," I said looking at Tigist. "How is this possible?"

I don't know, Danika. But we must leave, now, Tigist said, urging me to the door.

"It's unlocked," I said, turning the handle.

Good, let's go, Tigist said as we stepped into the hallway.

Immediately after stepping into the hallway, I heard something from the shadows. Looking around, I saw a jinn vanish after being hit by a katana that resembled the Nexus.

"You should be more careful, Danika," an entity said, stepping out from the shadows and slipping her katana into a sheath she wore on her back.

"You're very beautiful," I said, looking at the woman, rubbing my eyes because they went blurry again.

"Thank you," she responded smiling. "Don't you worry. The blurriness will fade soon," she said gently, touching my cheek. "Love yourself," she said as I saw a tear fall from her eye.

As I looked at her, I saw everything I wanted to be; she was perfect. She had beautiful black hair tied back in a single dutch french braid like my own, soft-toned white skin, with a couple visible tattoos. The small diamond stud earrings sparkled as the moonlight hit them, and her pearly white teeth shone as she smiled at me. As her hand gracefully left my cheek, she looked as if she wanted to say something but was holding back. As she began walking down the dark hall, she suddenly disappeared.

"I wonder who she was?" I asked, looking at Tigist. "I could hope for nothing more than to be just like her one day."

Don't worry, kiddo, you will, Tigist

"What do you mean?" I asked.

Child, I thought it would be obvious who that was, Tigist said, shaking her head.

"That was me," I said softly.

Yes, Tigist said.

"Damn! I'm hot," I said with a big smile. "But she seemed sad."

Danika, someone's coming, we need to go back into the cell, Tigist said.

It was then that I heard someone sneaking down the hallway. Cracking the door open again to take a look, I saw the boy from the showers holding a security guard in a headlock.

"Tigist, it's my dad," I said quietly.

Do something to get his attention, Tigist said.

"Help! Please help me," I said to the boy, but he did not hear me.

That's the best you can do? I thought you were such a great actress? Tigist asked.

"What do you want me to do?" I said, staring at Tigist.

Try harder, Tigist said.

"Sure, Yoda," I replied, mocking Tigist.

"Please help me!" I said louder after closing the door to the cell.

Yoda—I resent that, Tigist said, shaking her head. *He's so ugly, and I'm beautiful.*

"Where are you?" Jensen replied softly.

"Over here," I said.

"How did you get here?" he asked, looking through the small barred window of the door.

"I'm not sure," I said, confused about what to say next.

"I'm gonna get you out of there," he said as he flicked his wrist and the Nevillin appeared. He drove it downward into the lock of the door, snapping the lock.

"Oh, thank you so much," I said, pushing it open.

"What's your name?" he asked.

"Danika," I hesitatingly replied.

"That's a beautiful name. I'm Jensen," he said quietly. "How old are you?"

Lie to him. You look really young for your age, so he'll believe you, Tigist said.

"Fourteen," I replied nervously.

"Follow me, Danika," he said nodding, "and stay close."

I followed him down the dark, moonlit hallway until we came upon an open door. The room was very well lit. When we looked around the corner, it was then that I saw, sprawled out on a metal table, a nude boy who must've been aged around eleven or twelve.

Dressed in scrubs, two doctors walked in from another door into the room.

"Look at this kid. He was so scared he pissed himself," one of them laughed.

"Nasty," the other responded.

"Danika, listen to me. I have to go in there. You stay here. Can you do that?" Jensen asked.

"Yes, I can," I said.

When the Nevillin appeared, he also was holding a cross that was once a tattoo on his wrist.

"How'd you do that?" I asked, smiling.

"Magic," Jensen smiled, handing me the cross.

"The warden said she wanted this one done tonight, his organs removed and his blood fully drained. He's worth a lot to Mr. Natas," a guard said, walking into the room with the knocked-out boy.

"Is he an angel too?" one of the doctors mocked.

"No, he's a jinn."

Tigist, it's Dean. We have to help him, I said in my head concerned as the guard dropped Dean to the ground.

Just then, Jensen sprang into action. As he fought the guards, I saw the doctors running out of the room, and the alarm to the entire facility began to sound. Running after them, I caught up. I tripped them, and they fell to the ground.

"Who the hell is she?" one doctor said, looking at the other.

"She's just a little girl, what is she going to do?"

Just then they both ran at me. I was able to knock them both out after I'd deflected several of their weak attacks.

"Would you like to see your friends die, little one?" a big guard said from behind me before he grabbed my hair and yanked me backward.

"Freeze!" he shouted as Jensen came running around the corner. "Slowly, put your hands behind your head, and drop to your knees," he demanded of Jensen.

"Jensen," I said, acting scared as the guard once again yanked my hair.

"You're no SWAT team," Jensen sneered.

"Let's just say, we work for someone that is very interested in you and your friend," he said before he was stabbed from behind by a spear.

"Looks like you're the only one that'll be dropping to their knees today," Jensen said.

The guard dropped me, and I fell to the ground. Another member of the SWAT team engaged Jensen, while he was blocking everything they threw at him. He fought valiantly. Dean pulled the spear out of the big guard and then ran past me and killed another SWAT guy, but this one vanished like a jinn. Like lightning, Jensen ran at three of the others and cut the barrels off their guns with the Nevillin. Suddenly a dark being came at Jensen from out of nowhere, dressed in dark blue with a dark-red cloak. I watched as it flicked its wrist and a katana appeared. As Jensen fought hard against this dark being, I could tell it was highly trained in the martial arts and fencing. From out of nowhere, it threw a kick across Jensen's face. When he fell to the ground, it went in for a killer blow, but its katana was met by another.

"I don't think so, Rayne," the older version of me said, glaring at Rayne.

"I was wondering if you'd show up," Rayne said as she pointed the katana at her.

"Leave them be," the older version of me said in a threatening tone.

"Oh, Enreal," Rayne said before quickly flying at me, pointing her katana to my throat.

"How 'bout this, no doubt you and she have something very much in common. I wonder what would happen if I struck her down."

"You could try," Enreal said.

"As you wish, Your Highness," Rayne said as she swung her katana down at me, only to be blocked by Dean. "I didn't see that coming," Rayne said awkwardly, shocked.

"You'll see that I'm full of surprises," Dean said before Rayne kicked him across the room.

"Obviously, you didn't see that coming either," Enreal said, kicking Rayne to the ground.

"Jensen, get them out of here. I'll take it from here," Enreal said as Rayne got up off the floor.

"Where's the elder grimoire, Enreal? I know you stole it from us," Rayne said as their katanas met.

"Stole? How can you steal that which rightfully belongs to you?" Enreal said as she and Rayne began fighting.

"Jensen, there's the main entry door, down at the end of this hall," Dean said as we heard the sounds of katanas swiftly clanging together.

Looking around every corner, I saw that Eastlake had become a war zone. Teenagers were being slaughtered left and right.

Making our way carefully to the door, four men stepped out in front of us with guns drawn.

"Where do you think you're going?" one of the guards said, pointing a gun at us.

"Listen, man, just walk away, you don't need to do this," Dean said, trying to compromise.

"Lie down on the ground, and put your hands behind your heads," one of them said.

"I don't think so," Jensen replied.

Suddenly the men stepped back and began shooting. Jensen swung the Nevillin every which way, blocking the bullets. When I saw another man come out of the corner of my eye, I picked up a piece of debris from the ground and threw it at him. Hitting him right between the eyes, I turned around to see Jensen chop the hands of the shooters. But not before one last bullet rang out, hitting me in the abdomen. I had never felt such intense pain.

Danika! Tigist shouted in my head.

"Jensen . . . ," I said as I turned around, "something's wrong," then I stumbled.

Falling backward, I could feel someone had caught me.

"Danika, don't talk," Dean said quietly, holding me.

"How bad is it, Dean?" Jensen asked.

"It's bad. We have to get out of here," Dean said.

Opening up the corner of my shirt, I saw the look on Jensen's face and looked down, and I saw blood slowly oozing out from the bullet-size opening.

"I'm cold," I said, taking a deep breath.

"Jensen, she's in bad shape," Dean said, applying pressure to the wound.

"All right, follow me," Jensen said, bulldozing through anyone in his path.

Kicking the door open, we ran outside to see rain pouring down. I watched Jensen still fighting the jinn that came at him as Dean ran up to a truck.

"I gotta put you down, but only for a second," Dean said, putting me down as he elbowed the window and shattered it.

"What's wrong?" I asked, still applying pressure to the wound, as I saw Dean shake his head in disappointment.

"It was already unlocked," he said as I smiled and laughed in pain.

"Ah, don't make me laugh, it hurts," I said smiling and shaking my head.

Opening the back door, Dean helped me in as I lay down on the back seat. Holding my wound, I looked out the door to see Jensen still fighting a horde of jinn and keeping them away from the truck.

"Jensen!" Dean shouted. "We are leaving!"

"Go, go, go!" Jensen said, jumping into the back seat with me. I could feel the motion of the car as it sped off.

"Jensen," I said, taking a deep breath.

"Yeah," he responded, flicking his wrist and cutting his hand on the blade of the Nevillin.

When the blood began to run out of the cut on his hand, he let it drip into my wound. When it did nothing, he squeezed his hand tighter so more blood would flow out. But he looked on in frustration as nothing happened.

"This isn't happening. Why the hell isn't this working?" Jensen said frustrated.

"You should have this back," I said, putting the cross in his hand and holding it there. "You're gonna need it," I said as Jensen looked at me sadly.

"You keep it, Danika," Jensen said sadly.

"I'll keep it safe, Jensen," I said as I closed my eyes, holding the cross, and everything became dark.

The Shadow

Danika

Opening my eyes, I asked, "Are we dead?" Everywhere I looked, I saw darkness.

It'd take a lot more than a bullet to kill you. That . . . and I'm not sure you can even die in a time jump.

"How would you know, silly bird?" I asked, hearing Tigist flying around.

All of a sudden, the room we were in brightened up when Tigist found a switch and flicked it on. Everywhere I looked, I saw Middle East decor all over the room. Walking over to the desk in the room, I looked at some of the pictures, and in all of them I constantly saw one person.

Barack Al-Rashid, Tigist said as I picked up one of the pictures.

"This can't be right. What the hell are we doing here?" I said, looking at Tigist.

I believe we time-jumped within a time jump, Tigist said, confused and thinking.

"You mean, my body that got shot is still in that time with the younger version of my dad and we're back in the present day again?" I asked.

I'm not sure, Tigist said.

"This is the future?" I said.

Was that a question? Tigist asked.

"No, that was a statement. This is the future."

How do you know?

"Because when we originally left our time, this wasn't the

date," I said, showing Tigist a single picture that was lying on the desk.

What's your dad doing here? Tigist asked, looking at a picture they had of him as if he had been under surveillance by Barack.

"I have no idea," I said concerned.

So what are we doing here? Tigist asked.

"How am I supposed to know?" I said confused, looking at Tigist, who was also shrugging. "Quickly, hide, Tigist! Someone's coming," I said when I heard people talking just outside the room we were in.

"We sure do a lot of hiding," I said and rolled my eyes.

"Rayne, you said I could keep the American," I heard a man say.

"No, Barack! I said you could keep all but one," Rayne answered. "And seeing how you only have one and he just happens to be the one I'm looking for, he belongs to me."

"This is—" Barack said frustrated before being cut off.

"This is what?" Rayne said sternly. "Perhaps you feel you're being treated unfairly?" she asked, placing her hand on his shoulder.

"No," Barack said.

"Good," Rayne said. "Now bring me the American."

The doors opened to the office, and in walked two men holding the arms of a man that had a bag over his head.

"Dad," I whispered when they removed the bag from his head.

"Release him now!" I shouted, jumping up in their view and flicking my wrist.

Real subtle, Danika, Tigist said, flying up to the ceiling.

"We meet again," Rayne said as I looked at my dad. "Listen here, Danika," Rayne said, holding a small orb of some kind. "Lay down your katana. I'll only tell you once."

"No," I said as Rayne began tapping the orb against her leg.

"How come this thing isn't working?" Rayne said irritated.

"To think we're related, Rayne," my dad said and began laughing.

"Shut up," Rayne said, punching my dad across the face. "Danika," Rayne said softly, "such nuisance."

Flying across the room, I hit one of the men holding my dad

so hard he went flying out the window. Rayne then flicked her wrist, and a katana appeared. She quickly began attacking me. Then she allowed a horde of jinn and reapers to begin attacking me, and she backed off. I was fighting them off, and they were no match for my skill or speed. I cut my dad's restraints. He stood up, flicked his wrist, and began fighting the jinn and reapers with me. I saw Barack Al-Rashid escape to the roof of the building. When the jinn and reapers that had been attacking us were all dead, I knew we had to stop Rayne from getting Al-Rashid to safety.

"What was that orb?" I asked, looking at my dad.

"The orb was something created by the dark lord to disarm us. But you, Danika, are more powerful than any trinket they may possess, this is why it has no effect on you. Al-Rashid, besides Rayne, is the only one who knows where Rashad Natas is keeping Dean."

"Let's get him," I said before following my dad to the roof. "Dad, take this, it will deflect any evil thrown at you by the orb Rayne possesses," I said as we stood behind a door that said "Roof Access."

"My cross," Dad said, looking at it.

"I kept it safe, like I told you I would when I saw you at Eastlake," I said, taking a deep breath. "It's time for it to serve you once more."

"How do you know it will deflect the power of that orb?" Dad asked.

"I don't, but I believe in its power," I said.

"Thank you," he said, kissing me on the cheek before kicking the door open.

"Rayne!" Jensen shouted as Rayne pulled out the orb.

"What is wrong with this thing? Ah! Forget it! We'll finish this once and for all," Rayne shouted back at us.

"It doesn't have to be like this, Rayne. We could be a family again," Jensen shouted, trying to get through to her.

"One of us must die now, brother," Rayne said, circling around.

"I don't want to fight you," Jensen said.

"Then die!" Rayne shouted, swinging her katana.

From out of nowhere, a shadow fell from the sky, wielding a lightning bolt spear. Blocking the bolt as soon as it was swung at me, I went flying backward off the side of the roof.

"Danika!" Jensen shouted.

"Can't save them all," Rayne said as Jensen began to attack her.

Danika, wake up! Tigist shouted.

"Tigist, what's going on?" I asked as I was flying downward through the air. "Oh no!" I said, turning my body so my feet were downward.

Coming to a stop in midair, I shot back up in the air like a rocket.

"What was that with the lightning bolt spear?" I asked Tigist.

I have no idea, Tigist said.

I could see my dad fighting Rayne on the rooftop as I hovered in the air. I saw the shadow with the lightning bolt walking toward them as they fought. I watched as it grabbed Al-Rashid and threw him down onto the helicopter landing pad, breaking his legs. Without warning, the shadow with the lightning bolt spear flew up into the air and began to attack me. As we collided back and forth, I grabbed the shadow and threw it down to the landing pad. Lunging at it, I saw its face and immediately stopped.

"Dean?" I said, looking at him. "It is you. Why are you doing this?"

"I . . ." he stopped and thought. "What did they do to me?"

"Dean," my dad said, looking at us.

"Jensen," Dean said, looking at him. "Get away from me, Danika!" Dean shouted scared.

Getting up from the ground, Dean looked at Rayne. Quickly flying at her, he grabbed her and threw her into the helicopter hovering above us and it exploded.

"Dean," Jensen said, looking at him.

"You're not safe with me," Dean responded.

Suddenly Rayne came from out of nowhere and kicked Dean off the side of the building. I quickly flew after him. I grabbed him just before he was about to hit the ground, and then everything went dark.

***

It was early morning. The sun was warm as it shone down through my bedroom window. The house smelled of fresh, brewing coffee. I could hear Nikki downstairs talking to someone. Jumping out of bed quickly, Tigist and I looked around my room to see if anything had possibly changed.

Everything seems to be the way you left it, Tigist said.

"Not really, these clothes aren't mine," I said, picking up a shirt that was on the dresser and putting it to my nose.

"These smell like Valerie's clothes," I said.

As I walked through the hallway to go downstairs, I gently touched the pictures, feeling the Braille at the bottom of the frame that Nikki put on them when I was blind so I'd know the picture and remember the story of that day. Smiling, I remembered that story of a very loved young girl. Walking downstairs, I suddenly heard a voice from behind me.

"Danika," the raspy voice said.

"Dad," I said, turning around and lunging into his arms, hugging him.

"You look as beautiful as when I last saw you," he said, looking at me.

"It wasn't that long ago, Dad," I said and smiled.

"I know," he said, looking at me smiling.

"How's Dean?" I asked.

"I never found him," he said saddened.

"Nikki," I said as she walked in the room.

"Oh my gosh, sweetheart, look at you," Nikki said, hugging and kissing me.

"Danika," a voice said from behind me.

"Valerie," I said, turning around and taking a deep breath to keep me from being overwhelmed.

"Hey you," she added, smiling and trying not to cry.

"Hey back," I said, walking up to her and kissing her. "I'll never leave your side again," I said while I hugged her.

As my parents prepared dinner, Valerie and I went upstairs in my room to talk. In our conversation, I discovered that Valerie had come out to her parents about her being gay. They told her they needed time to process this as it was a great disappointment to them both. My grandmother, stricken with grief and disappointment, chose to move out.

With prom only a couple of weeks away, Valerie and I enjoyed our time together and couldn't wait for the day to finally be here.

Valerie

The next morning was so beautiful. The sun was warm and bright. The weather was perfect for surfing. Danika and I grabbed our boards and headed to the ocean. After several hours of surfing the beautiful waves, Danika and I decided to sit and enjoy the lunch we'd packed. Looking at Danika, I felt shivers run down my body. I was so in love with her. Sitting up on my knees, I leaned in toward her and rested my forehead against hers, softly closing my eyes. I felt Danika run her fingers through my hair before we both smiled and shared a kiss.

"I got it," we heard a voice say.

"What's up, Matt?" I said.

"Nothing. But that picture came out fantastic. I'll make sure to get you a copy."

Prom Night

Valerie

The day finally came. I couldn't wait to go to senior prom with Danika. I had goose bumps throughout the day just counting the minutes before I could take her to prom. My dress was beautiful. It was a dark burgundy dress with lace straps.

"You look beautiful," Mr. Kane said, walking into the living room and seeing me in my dress.

"Thank you, Mr. Kane," I said.

"So the limousine should be here soon," Mr. Kane said as Danika came out of the bathroom.

"Never in my life have I seen anyone so beautiful," I said, anxiously biting my lower lip and smiling as I looked at Danika.

She was wearing a light-blue dress with handmade flowers that beaded off her shoulders.

"You look gorgeous," I said, giving Danika a kiss and putting my arms around her.

"So do you," Danika said kissing me on the lips.

"You girls both look so beautiful," Nikki said and smiled before hugging us both.

When the limousine pulled up, our friends hopped out as their parents pulled up behind the limo. Everyone came inside as Danika's parents hosted a little get-together for our friends and their parents. What we didn't expect was for my parents to show up.

"What are you guys doing here?" I asked them as Mr. Kane walked up behind me.

"Valerie, we were . . . ," my mother said, before pausing as Danika walked up.

"George, Shirley, it's so nice to see you again. Won't you come inside and join us?" Danika said as if she knew they'd be here.

"You did this?" I whispered to Danika.

"I did. I promise, everything's going to be perfect," she said as I smiled and kissed her on the cheek.

"Danika, thank you so much for inviting us," George said as Danika draped her arm through his and showed them both into the house.

"George, Shirley, these are my parents, Jensen and Nikki," Danika said, introducing them.

"Pleasure to meet you," Jensen said, shaking George's hand and then Shirley's.

"Welcome to our home," Nikki said, also shaking their hands. "Can I get you something to drink?"

"Yes please," Shirley responded. "How far along are you?"

"Six months," Nikki responded.

"Do you know the sex?" Shirley asked.

"No, we want it to be a surprise," Nikki said.

"Do you have names picked out?"

"Samuel if it's a boy, Trinity if it's a girl."

"Beautiful names," Shirley said and smiled.

"Thank you," Nikki said.

"So, Jensen, Danika tells me you're in the military?" George asked, looking at Jensen.

"Delta Force."

"Delta Force! Wow," George said, "very impressive."

"Yeah, I've been in for as long as I can remember," Jensen said as George looked at a picture of Octavia's cover of *Razorblade Kiss* on the wall.

"Wow," George said, "your wife, Octavia, did so many wonderful things. I was sad to hear she passed away." He and I looked at a picture of Octavia holding the *Metal Reigns* magazine that had done a spread on her after she appeared on the *Metal Reigns* talk show.

"She was an amazing person," Jensen said, thinking back on fond memories. "You know, your daughter there is pretty amazing herself. She may be going to Juilliard on a scholarship."

"Yes, we're very proud of her," George said. "It was this, coming out thing that really floored her mother and I. The thought of not having some grandchildren was very disappointing."

"As long as the girls are happy. That's all that should matter," Jensen said.

"I suppose you're right."

After watching Danika interact with my parents, I could see that they genuinely liked her. We wrapped everything up and took pictures with our dates. Shortly after, my parents pulled me aside to talk.

"Would you like to come home, sweetheart?" my mom asked.

"I want to hear you say that you'll love me despite my choices. You don't like that I'm gay, but I am, and I won't apologize for it." Then I said, looking at Danika, "I love her, Mom."

"Honey, we love you with all our hearts, and Danika is a splendid girl. We just hope she knows how lucky she is to have you," my mom said.

"We're lucky to have each other," I said.

"Everyone's ready to get going," Danika said, walking up to my parents and I. "I'm so glad you both came," she said, hugging my mom and dad.

"Thank you for inviting us, Danika," Shirley said smiling before she turned around and kissed me on the cheek.

"I'll see you in the limo," Danika said, smiling and squeezing my hand softly before walking out to the limo.

"Valerie, we're very proud of you. This came for you from Juilliard, today," my dad said.

"Oh my god, you don't think it could be my acceptance letter?" I asked my parents.

"I think it is," my mother said.

"I can't open it now. If it's bad news, I don't want it to wreck my prom night with Danika," I said, putting it in the small purse I had brought. "I'll open it tomorrow. Thank you both so much. I love you," I said, hugging them at the same time.

When we arrived at the Phoenix Club in Anaheim, we were greeted at the front door and had our picture taken in front of a dark-blue canvas.

"That came out wonderful, girls," one of the teachers who was standing behind the photographer said.

"Thank you, Mr. Sullivan," I said.

"I can't believe the school board allowed that," another teacher said, talking to Mr. Sullivan.

"Well, Mrs. Beatty, they didn't do anything wrong, and they were permitted to attend together as a couple," Mr. Sullivan said.

"God judges sinners," Mrs. Beatty said adamantly.

"Excuse me," Danika said, getting Mrs. Beatty's attention.

"Yes, dear?" she asked.

"How is it that you can pass judgement so easily?" Danika asked.

"I'm sorry?" Mrs. Beatty asked confused.

"I heard your trite remark. So I'll ask you again, what right do you have to pass judgment on us?" Danika asked.

"What you are doing is an abomination to God," she said.

"Are you sure about that?" Danika asked and smirked.

"These are the facts, honey," she said, smirking back.

"Facts . . . really? What if I told you, that was a typo and should have never made it into the Good Book?" Danika asked.

"Blasphemy," Mrs. Beatty said offended. "You should be ashamed of yourself, Danika."

"Mrs. Beatty, in the end, when all this is gone and doesn't exist anymore, I'll be accepting your apology after you beg for forgiveness," Danika said before walking away. "Have a nice night."

Walking in the front door of the club, it was just as I imagined. There was a float on one side of the room holding streamers. There were all sorts of beautiful decorations everywhere I looked. I smiled and thought, *What could be better than this?*

"Danika, come, let's dance," I said, taking her hand and pulling her out onto the dance floor.

Danika

After a few songs and some dancing, we found our table. Not long after our dinner arrived, a ballot came to our table asking to cast votes for the prom king and queen.

When it came time to crown the king and queen, the hair on the back of my neck stood up.

"Justin Cole is our king, and . . . Valerie Hammond is our

queen," a boy onstage announced.

When the song "Something about the Way You Look Tonight" came on, Justin politely walked offstage and took my hand and escorted me to Valerie. He also went and invited his date, Ashley, to dance. Valerie took me in her arms. The way she danced with me, it was as if no one else in the world existed, and every now and then she kissed me softly on the neck.

When the prom ended and we were in the limo on the way home, Bastian came up with the idea that we should not end the night so quickly but go home, change, and regroup for a night of more fun.

"Let's all keep in contact, and we'll meet up in front of Killer Dana surf shop," Bastian said to all of us.

"Cool," Valerie said.

***

After about an hour, we all met in front of Killer Dana. It was around twelve midnight.

"So what should we do?" I asked.

"Let's roll down to Circle K and grab some cigars and beers and go to the beach and do some night surfing. Trent is working, he'll hook us up with the beer," Bastian said.

When we got to Circle K, we met with some other friends we knew from school. As Bastian was leaning up against their car talking to them, suddenly five Hispanic hoodlums walked around the corner.

"Valerie, get back into the car," I said when I saw them.

"Did you say something, punk?" one of them said mad. He was walking up to us with his hands behind his back.

"Nobody said anything to you," Bastian said, turning to face them.

"You talking smack, fool?" another one said.

"No. Why don't we all just go about our business. We're not looking for trouble," Justin said.

"Well, you found trouble, *ese!*" one of them said, jumping past his friend to hit Bastian in the face.

"Ashley, get in the car!" I demanded before she quickly got in and locked the doors.

Running up to one of them and throwing him up against the side of the convenient store, I watched as the glass shattered and came crashing down. As Bastian and Justin ran to the more spacious part of the parking lot, the hoodlums went after them except one.

"You should have locked yourself in the car too," one of them said, walking up to me.

Swinging punch after punch, I dodged all his weak attempts with little effort before I pushed him to the ground and showed him the Nexus. Immediately after seeing the Nexus, he took off running like a coward.

Running over to help Bastian and Justin, I began pulling them off and throwing them to the ground. That was when I heard Valerie scream. I turned to see that one of the hoodlums had broken the window of the car and was trying to grab Valerie. As soon as I got to him and threw him to the ground, from out of nowhere I was suddenly being attacked by a shadow that carried the lightning bolt and wielded it as a sword.

"Dean, you must snap out of it. I'm your niece, Danika," I said before flicking my wrist.

"I'm not Dean," a female voice said.

Fighting long and hard, she stopped and looked at me. Turning her head, she looked at Valerie before removing the hood and revealing her face.

"You're beautiful," I said. "Who are you?"

"A relic of the past," she said.

"I apologize for my actions," she said before flying off into the sky.

Flicking my wrist, I looked over to see Bastian, Justin, and three of the Hispanic guys standing there looking at me. It's as if the Hispanic guys had forgotten about what they were fighting with us for. They looked at one another and took off running.

"Are you guys okay?" Trent asked, coming out of the convenience store. "The cops should be here any minute."

"What a friend you are, bro. Don't even come out here to help as you could see us being attacked," Bastian shouted at Trent.

"Bastian, I called the police," Trent said.

"Whatever!" Bastian replied.

"Bastian, that's enough. Simmer down!" I shouted.

Just then the police came pulling up with their sirens and lights blaring.

"You kids all right?" an officer asked me as he got out of his car.

"Yes," Bastian said.

"What are you kids doing out this late?" the officer asked.

"We were just hanging out, Officer," Valerie said.

"See, Bastian, I told you I called them," Trent said.

"Shut the hell up, Trent!" Bastian shouted.

"I ought to kick your ass, Bastian," Trent said mad.

"You can try," Bastian said as he lunged at him and one of the officers caught him.

"Listen, your friend over there is real close to getting arrested. I want you to get him in the car and go home," the officer said to me.

"I understand, Officer," I responded.

After getting Bastian in the car and taking him home, Valerie and I went home.

In my bedroom, we got comfortable in some beautiful lingerie, and Valerie began playing her cello very softly.

"So I found this in your purse," I said, holding up the envelope Valerie had gotten from Juilliard.

"I'm scared to open it," Valerie said.

"Don't be scared. This is your future, and you've worked hard all four years at Dana Hills to see this come to fruition."

"What if I don't get in?" Valerie said hesitantly.

"Why don't you open it and we'll find out together if our future has us living in New York . . ." I said as Valerie cut me off.

"You'll come with me?" Valerie asked.

"I'm never going to leave your side for anything," I said. "I love you more than anything."

"I love you too," Valerie said, taking a deep breath. "Here goes nothing," Valerie said, ripping the envelope and taking the paper out.

Suddenly the look on Valerie's face went pale. I immediately felt horrible for her as she looked at me.

"What is it?" I asked as she shook her head.

"Do you like the Yankees?" Valerie asked and smiled.

"I do now!" I said, excited for her and smiling so big it hurt.

We hugged one another. Taking my hand, Valerie invited me to sit with my back toward her in the seat as she took my hands and continued to play the cello. Softly she began kissing my neck till our lips met.

Serial Killer

Danika

It wasn't long after prom that Valerie and I graduated from school as valedictorians, with Valerie set to attend Juilliard. I proposed the idea to my father to regroup Embrace the Fate, with me filling in my mother's shoes as lead singer. We were putting out a new CD and following it with a tour. I already knew all the songs of Embrace the Fate and could hit all the same octaves as my mother. My father agreed and got everyone back together, but Dean's absence was highly felt by everyone. My friend Jimmy took over the drums in Dean's absence, and it didn't take long for us to record an album. Kicking off the tour, we started in Las Vegas, and would be the first band to ever play at the new Raiders stadium.

Jensen

As soon as we got to town, we checked into our room, and Nikki turned on the TV.

There was a news broadcast on television:

This just in. The serial killer calling himself Pyro hijacked another bus yesterday. In the attack, he burned four of his victims alive with three of the victims in critical condition and one dead. Pyro remains at large, and no one knows where he might strike next. Authorities are urging anyone who rides transit to remain on high alert and report anything that may look suspicious.

Also, Majid El-Khatib, caliphate to the Muslim regime, has finally finished his campaign of bringing about a peace treaty that will see the Middle East at peace with the world.

El-Khatib is also in the final stages of constructing a third temple, which is located on the Temple Mount, with it only a few months away from being completed. Religious scholars fear that the world has entered its final stage of judgment.

"What's the world coming to?" Nikki said aloud, taking a deep breath and shaking her head. "Why four victims?"

"Because he's done it four times," I said, walking into the room. "He adds a victim every time he strikes. So the next time there will be five victims."

"Jensen, how do you know these things?" Nikki asked, kissing me.

"I don't know," I responded. "I'm more shocked by the construction of that third temple in Jerusalem."

"Why?" Nikki asked.

"The last mission I was on, Majid said something about building a third temple, but I didn't put much thought into it till now. The Bible warns that when the third temple is built, this will bring about the apocalypse," I said.

"Yeah, but . . ." Nikki shrugged, "don't you think we'd already see signs of this?"

"With Danika here now, there's no telling when that apocalypse will come," I said, pausing and thinking. "We should get going, we're supposed to meet the kids for dinner," I said before touching Nikki's stomach.

***

Danika

"I was thinking, after dinner we could go to the strip," I said, looking at Valerie.

"That sounds like fun," Valerie said and smiled.

After dinner with my parents, Valerie and I went to the strip and had so much fun. We partied in the Hakkasan nightclub at the MGM and rode the roller coasters at the top of the Stratosphere. At about three in the morning, we decided to go back to the hotel, but we couldn't seem to get a cab or an Uber.

"Let's take the city bus, the Mandalay Bay isn't that far away,"

I said as we walked. "This way we can cruise down the strip."

"Are you happy?" Valerie asked as we came to the bus stop and waited.

"Of course I am," I said confused. "Why do you ask?"

"I just want to make sure," Valerie said smiling as the bus pulled up to the stop.

"With you by my side, Valerie, I'll always be happy," I said, taking her hands in mine.

"I don't want you to regret moving to New York with me," Valerie said.

"I regret nothing. Wherever you are, that's where I want to be," I said, kissing her.

After boarding the bus and finding a place to sit, we talked more about the concert tomorrow night. Not long after we boarded the city bus, it came to another stop. I looked out the window, and I saw a man with burn marks on his hands and face. He was wearing a beige trench coat, and looked very out of place. When he boarded the bus, he sat and began looking at everyone as if he were searching for something or someone. As he set his eyes on Valerie, I glared at him. But instead of averting his eyes, he continued to stare.

Danika, there's something really wrong here. We need to get off this bus, Tigist said, echoing in my head.

"Valerie, we're getting off at the next stop," I said quietly in her ear.

"What's wrong?" Valerie whispered.

"I'm not sure," I said as the bus came to a stop and the doors opened.

Taking Valerie's hand, we got up and began walking to the door.

"Dykes," the man whispered under his breath.

"Excuse me?" Valerie scoffed.

"Babe, let's go," I said, staring back at him as he glared at me.

"You're not going anywhere!" he shouted, pointing a gun at everyone on the bus. "Now everyone sit the hell down. You, driver, shut those doors and get this bus moving. All stops are now been canceled."

"Why are you doing this?" I asked calmly as he pointed the gun at me and the bus started moving.

"It's personal," he said.

"Are you sure? Because taking a bus full of innocent people as hostages does seem personal," I said, looking at him as he pointed the gun at Valerie.

"What do you know?" he said.

"It looks like you have a vendetta against the world, John Avery," I said as he continued pointing the gun at Valerie.

"How do you know my name?" he asked.

"I know lots of things, John," I said calmly.

"Where did you hear that name?" he asked again.

"Lucky guess?" I said and shrugged.

"That was no guess," he said.

"You don't have to do this," I said, looking at him. "It's vengeance you seek, but it isn't here," I said, pointing at everyone on the bus.

Walking up to him and putting my hand gently on his chest, I said, "For how could I forgive you if you haven't forgiven yourself?"

"I used to have a voice that sounded just like yours. It would tell me of the love I had for my family and my faith. But that's over now, a memory I wish to forget," John said.

"Our memories are all we have, John. What happened to your family wasn't your fault," I said, remaining calm.

"Sit down," he said, suddenly pushing me into my seat. "I will choose five of you, and the rest will bear witness and tell of it later. For I am Pyro, and I've come to extract my vengeance upon you."

"I tried," I whispered to Valerie.

"I know you did," Valerie said worried. "How bad is it going to get?"

"For him . . . the consequences will be severe."

Walking around the bus, he chose his five. Valerie and I were two of the five chosen.

"John Avery, before you go and make the biggest mistake of your life, you should take a moment and listen," I said as we all were on our knees in front of him.

"What the hell are you babbling about now, girl?" he said, looking at me.

"Listen," I said firmly, shutting my eyes. "Do you hear the

voice?"

"That's strange. I do," he replied.

"What does it say, John?" I asked.

"It says to kill you first," he said, grabbing me and pulling me away from the group.

"Then I guess you better do as it says," I said, looking at him down on my knees.

"Danika!" Valerie shouted scared.

"It's okay," I said. "I'm ready, John," I said, closing my eyes.

"It's nothing personal," he said as from out of his overcoat's sleeve he took out a rubber hose and dosed me in gasoline. I saw Valerie freaking out and upset as he lit a match. Then she lunged to tackle him. I saw the people on the bus holding her back.

"Remember, I warned you, John Avery," I said as he threw the lit match.

My body immediately went up in flames. Everyone on the bus was terrified and screaming until I stood up still covered in flames. Slowly I put my hands out in front of me and began consolidating and harnessing the flames till my body was no longer on fire and what remained was a ball of fire between the palms of my hands. Everyone watched in amazement. Pyro began to panic and throw more gasoline at me. But this was no use, he grabbed Valerie instead and ran out the door. Flicking my wrist, the ball of fire disappeared. When I pursued him, suddenly there were jinn everywhere, as if he was being protected. As soon as I flicked my wrist and the Nexus appeared, I saw the bus pull away as the passengers had forgotten what had happened when they looked upon the Nexus. When I looked down, I saw that I was wearing something completely different from what I had on.

"Well, you're still not much to look at," a woman around my dad's age said, walking up to me from out of the shadows.

"Rayne," I said.

"Call me Auntie," she said before swinging a katana at me.

Suddenly and without warning, a horde of jinn and reapers surrounded me and engaged all at once. I flicked my wrist, and when Tigist appeared, she flapped her wings, and before my eyes she became a beautiful long-bladed sword with a gold handle. Taking a place at my side, the sword pointed at my enemies. With little effort, all I had to do was think where I wanted the sword to go and it would do so.

From out of the sky, a winged shadow being descended and approached. As the jinn and reapers looked up at the sky, they all took a knee and bowed their heads, including Rayne. When the winged shadow being hit the ground, it approached me. Its face was hidden in the darkness of the black hooded cloak it was wearing.

Tigist once again changed form and perched herself on my forearm.

"Who are you?" I asked.

"Better question is, who are you?" the being asked in a scratchy voice.

"I'm Danika Kane," I said without fear.

"Yes, you are. You belong with me, Danika," it said. "You belong by my side."

"And you are?"

"I go by many names," it replied.

"Why would you think I belong with you?"

"We are the same, Danika. For now take this, and in time you'll use it for a good purpose," it said, handing me a Trivium blade.

"Why are you giving me this?"

"Go in peace, Danika Kane," it said as it ordered its army of jinn and reapers away.

***

Valerie

I woke up to the sound of pouring rain. I could not tell what the time was. When I looked out the small window, it was overcast, and there were dark clouds all over the sky. My hands and feet were bound, and wherever I was, it was dirty and grimy, and it smelled of mildew. I tried everything to get my hands and feet free. Suddenly the door at the top of a staircase opened, and down came John Avery.

"You can't keep me here!" I shouted, but he didn't respond. "Do you hear me, you psycho?"

"You're wrong," he said, setting a plate of food that he was holding on a table before touching my leg seductively. "I can do whatever I want."

"Screw you, pervert!" I shouted, spitting in his face.

"You need to learn some manners," he said, grabbing my face and forcing me to look at him. "You will learn," he said, pulling the handcuffs and dragging me to another room.

***

Danika

"Tigist, this isn't the direction he took her," I said.

I know, we need to find that bus so I can pick up his scent, Tigist responded.

"There's the bus," I said as we flew overhead.

Flying down fast, I hit the ground standing in front of the bus. The driver slammed on the brakes and stopped on a dime. Tigist came down and landed on my forearm. I could see the look in the people's eyes aboard the bus when they saw us.

"Mommy, look at the owl," a little girl said as we walked onto the bus. "She's pretty," the girl said, sticking her hand out to pet Tigist.

"Honey, no!" her mother said.

"It's okay, ma'am. Tigist loves to be pet," I said as the little girl pet Tigist.

I got it, Danika. I have his scent, Tigist said.

"You look so familiar," a young man on the bus said.

"You do look familiar," someone else commented.

"Maybe we knew each other in a past life," another man said. "Déjà vu."

"Maybe," I said smiling before walking off the bus.

"She's really pretty, Mom," the little girl said again to her mother. "I love her hair."

***

Valerie

Waking up light-headed, I squinted a few times before I could open my eyes completely. Looking around, I saw that everywhere I looked was brightly lit. I was lying on what felt like a table of bare metal. I was naked and cold. I continued to look around. My hands were handcuffed above my head as well as my feet to each side of the metal table. I struggled every which way to break free, until John Avery walked in the room. I'd never been so scared in my entire life as I was in this moment.

"Let me go, you freak!" I shouted.

"No more," he said, walking over to me with a ball gag. "Open your mouth," he continued as he tried putting the gag in my mouth. "If you don't take the gag," he said, showing me a hammer, "I'll bust all those beautiful pearly whites out of your mouth." I began to cry. "There, there. Don't cry, this will just last as long as you make it," he said, running his finger up the side of my thigh and showing me the ball gag.

"Don't touch me," I pleaded and cried.

"Touch you? The real fun hasn't even begun yet," he said, grabbing my face and forcing me to look at him again.

"What do you want from me?" I asked before I suddenly heard footsteps coming from above.

"What is that?" he said, looking up at the ceiling.

"Tigist," I said as she flew in and spread her wings out, covering my nude body as the ceiling caved in like an explosion with no fire.

There in front of me I saw Danika, but she was unlike I'd ever seen her before. She was wearing what looked like an armor, but it was tight to her skin, and she had a black gauntlet on her right forearm.

"You," he said, quickly scrambling to get to me, but when he did, Tigist hit him across the face with her wing.

"It's over," Danika said, grabbing him as he fell backward.

Suddenly he pulled out what looked like a detonator.

"And what are you planning on doing with that?" Danika asked.

"I'm going to blow you and your girlfriend straight to hell," John said like a madman.

"When are you going to learn?" Danika said smiling.

"What are you?" John said frightened.

"Something you will never be able to comprehend," Danika said as she walked up to him.

"And why's that?" he asked.

"Because you're too stupid to ever understand," Danika said as he dropped his guard. "I have something that belongs to you, I wanted to give it back."

At that moment, Danika gently kissed her index finger and middle finger and touched his forehead, and just like that he went up in flames before he eventually disappeared.

"Danika," I said, lying there on the metal table, "where did he go?"

"Somewhere he will no longer be able to hurt anyone again," Danika said, unfazed by what just happened.

"Is he dead?" I asked.

"Let's not talk about that," Danika said, walking over to the table where I was tied up.

"Thank you, Tigist," I said gratefully to Tigist as she flew off the table.

"Why are you looking at me like that?" I asked as I looked at Danika, and she smiled. "It's really cold in here," I said.

"I can see that," Danika said, smiling flirtatiously. "Maybe I should just leave you handcuffed."

"Really, Danika?" I said unamused.

"You're right, we'll take the handcuffs with us," Danika said as we both laughed.

"I love you so much," Danika said smiling before kissing me on the lips and placing her hand on the cuffs. As she uncuffed me, Danika said, "Let's go home."

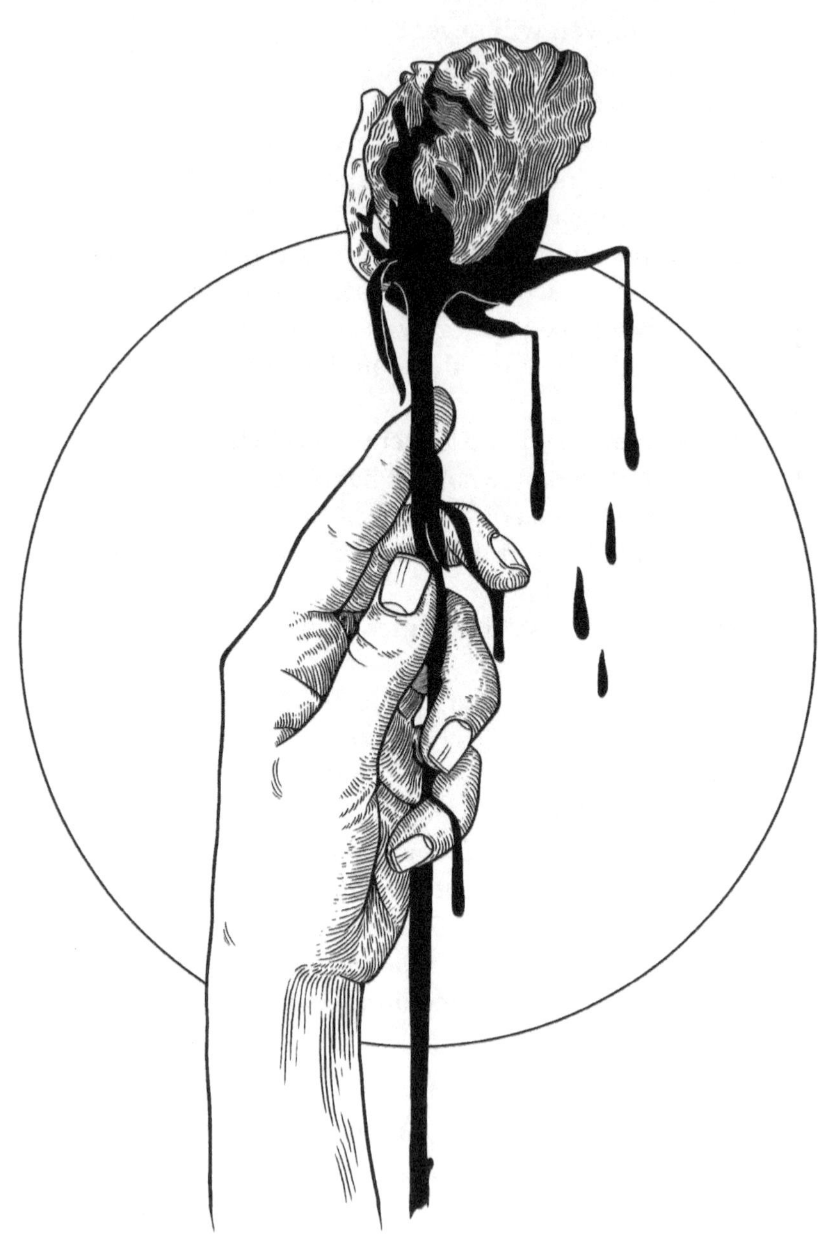

Beautiful Engagement

Valerie

After touring for six months, we decided to take a two-month break and stay in Las Vegas. As I walked through the Galleria mall in Henderson, I continued to look in every jewelry store to find the perfect ring. I loved Danika so much. I knew I wanted to spend the rest of my life with her. I got everything planned out in my head, and I knew how I was going to ask her to marry me. But I could not find one ring that looked like something she'd love. I searched already for months, high and low for the perfect ring till I came to a jewelry store called Ultra Diamonds—and there it was. Sitting on top of a small cushioned pedestal, it was like it had just been there waiting for me. The way I saw it, it drew me in to look closer. It was beautiful, and I knew Danika would love it. It was platinum gold with beautiful Celtic knots throughout the sides. It had five small baguette diamonds placed in the white gold on each side of the diamond in the middle.

"Can I help you?" a lady asked.

"Can I see that ring please?" I asked, pointing to it.

"Maybe you should stay over here and look in this case," the lady said.

"Why?" I asked.

"Because, dear, that specific ring you're looking at costs more than you can afford," the lady said.

"Really," I said frustrated. "You sure about that?"

"Yes."

"Do you work on commission?" I asked.

"Not that it's any of your business, but yes," the lady said with an attitude.

"Awesome," I said politely. "Thank you."

Walking further around the mall, I looked at several different jewelry stores for the same ring, but I found nothing that compared to the ring I saw at Ultra Diamonds. So I decided to go back. Walking back over to Ultra Diamonds, I saw Maya walking into Macy's.

"Hi, Maya," I said, catching up to her.

"Valerie," Maya said, looking at me oddly. "How are you?"

"I'm good," I said. "How are you?"

"Good," Maya said. "Where's Danika?"

"She doesn't know I'm here," I said. "I didn't know that you were still in Vegas."

"I am, but only for a couple more days," Maya said.

"I see," I said, shaking my head and thinking. "Can I get your opinion on something?" I asked Maya.

"Sure," Maya said, walking with me to Ultra Diamonds.

"Back again, huh?" the lady from before commented.

"Yep," I said, "it's me."

"Can I show you anything?" the lady asked, patronizing.

"Nope, just looking," I said as she walked away.

"Why didn't you have her help you?" Maya asked.

"It's a long story," I responded.

"We're ready," I said when I saw a pretty young woman with short dark-brown hair and a polka dot dress walk out from the back.

"My name is Amanda," she said politely. "Can I help you?"

"I'd like to see that ring right there please," I said, pointing to the ring I asked to see earlier.

"Sure," she said, getting a jewelry cushion out.

Taking it out of the cabinet, she handed it to me, along with a magnifying glass so I could examine the clarity.

"What do you think?" I asked Maya, showing her the ring.

"I think Danika will love it," Maya said, looking at it closely with the magnifying glass.

"That makes me so happy," I said.

"When were you thinking of popping the question?" Maya asked.

"We have a concert in two weeks at the T-Mobile Arena.

When I come out to sing 'True Love' with her, I'm going to ask her."

"That sounds beautiful," Maya said. "Danika will be so happy."

"I'll take the ring," I said turning to Amanda.

"Not sure if you're interested or not, but have you seen the matching necklace and bracelet?" Amanda said and smiled, showing it to us.

"I haven't," I said, looking at the necklace and bracelet. "They're beautiful."

"The things we'll do for the ones we love," Maya said. "Would you care to have lunch with me, Valerie?"

"I'd love to," I responded. "Amanda, I'm going to have lunch, and then I'm going to be right back to pay and pick up the ring, bracelet, and necklace."

"So you've decided on all of it?" Amanda asked.

"Yes, these are the things we do for the people we love most," I said, looking at Maya and smiling.

"That sounds great. I'll have everything cleaned up and packaged for you by the time you return," Amanda said. "One more thing, dear."

"What's that?" I asked.

"Do I know you from somewhere?" Amanda asked.

"I'm not sure, do you?"

"You look so familiar," Amanda said thinking.

"I just got one of those faces, I guess."

"Well, maybe it will come to me soon. Perhaps when you come back, I'll have remembered where."

"Perhaps," I said and smiled. "I'll see you soon."

During lunch with Maya, we talked about many wonderful things, and I was very happy to have finally gotten to know her. She was especially surprised when I told her of the house Danika and I bought in the Niguel Shores and that we'd be leaving for New York soon so I could attend Juilliard.

"We'll take the check please," I told the waiter as he pulled it out and handed it to Maya.

"Please, Maya, allow me," I said, reaching out for her to give me the bill.

"No, Valerie, it's my treat," Maya said, insisting.

"Fine, but you must come over to the house soon. I know Danika would love to see you," I said.

"You think so?" Maya asked. "She and I didn't exactly part on good terms."

"Nevertheless, I'm sure she'd love to see you," I said.

"I'll make it a point to see her soon," Maya said before we hugged. "Oh, one more thing," Maya smiled, "congratulations on Juilliard."

"Thank you." I smiled before we walked off in separate directions.

Once back at the Ultra Diamonds, I was first met by the lady who was rude to me earlier.

"Hello. I'd like to speak to Amanda please," I said.

"She's busy with someone else at the moment."

"Excuse me," a girl, around thirteen, said while walking up to me.

"Yes?" I said, looking at her and seeing she was wearing an Embrace the Fate T-shirt. "Nice shirt."

"You're Valerie Hammond, the cello player of Embrace the Fate, right?" the girl asked as if she already knew.

"I am," I replied.

"My name is Brittney. I'm your biggest fan. Can you sign my shirt?" Brittney asked excitedly.

"Sure," I said as she handed me a Sharpie and I signed the back of her shirt. "Brittney, are you going to the concert in the next couple weeks at the T-Mobile Arena?"

"No, my parents can't afford it unfortunately," the girl said sadly.

"Are you here with your parents?" I asked.

"Yeah, right over there," she said as I looked up and saw her parents give me a small wave and smile.

"Hello," I said, greeting her parents and shaking their hands.

"Valerie Hammond, it is such a pleasure to meet you. I'm Julie, and this is my husband, Mark. We've been listening to Embrace the Fate for years. Octavia's voice was just amazing, and when Danika sings, it is as if her mother is possessing her vocal cords."

"I'm so happy to hear you say that," I said. "There's nothing Danika strives toward more than making her mom proud," I said and smiled. "Listen, Brittney shared with me that it's always been a dream of your family's to attend one of our concerts."

"It has, but it's always been really tough to afford," Julie said.

"Well, I'm going to make that dream come true," I said, handing them the business card of Pierce Hatchet. "Pierce will be expecting your call. He will give you the tickets to the show. I will see to it that your family has front-row seats."

"Oh my gosh, really?" Brittney said in excitement.

"Really," I repeated as Brittney hugged me.

"Thank you so much, Valerie," Mark said.

"It's my pleasure," I said and smiled. "Brittney, what is your favorite song?"

"'True Love,'" Brittney replied.

"That one's my favorite too," I said smiling before bidding them farewell.

Walking back into Ultra Diamonds, Amanda greeted me with a smile.

"Hi, Amanda," I said politely.

"I knew you looked familiar, Embrace the Fate!" Amanda said. "I went to you guys' show when you played in New York at Madison Square Garden," she continued smiling. "I'm going to get your jewelry from the back. I'll be right back," Amanda said, walking to the back of the store smiling.

"Embrace the Fate, that operatic metal band," the rude lady said.

"That's the one," I said, looking at her and leaning forward. "Now you're thinking maybe you shouldn't have judged the book by its cover, huh?"

"All done," Amanda said, walking out from the back and to her register. "Okay, and the total is $32,782. Will that be cash or credit?"

"With which do you make a bigger commission?" I asked as the rude girl looked on.

"Honestly, I make the same with either," Amanda smiled.

"I'll put it on my credit card," I said, handing it to her. "And this is for you," I said as I handed her five hundred dollars in cash when she gave me back my card.

"Oh my gosh, thank you so much, I appreciate it," Amanda said very gratefully.

"No. I appreciate you, Amanda."

***

Two weeks passed by fast, and as the evening of the concert drew closer, we were all scrambling to get ready. As usual, the only two that were completely calm and collected were Danika and Jensen. I saw Jensen getting ready to make his entrance out onto the stage.

"You okay, babe?" Danika asked gently, kissing me on the back of the neck.

"Yeah. Listen to that crowd go wild seeing Jensen go out there," I said as Danika took my hand.

"You've never been this nervous before," Danika said again.

"I'll be fine," I said and smiled.

"I better get out there," Danika said as she kissed me. "I love you."

"I love you too," I said back to her. "Before you go, see that girl up front there? She was the one I met at the mall a couple of weeks ago," I said, pointing to Brittney in the front row.

"Yeah she was the one Pierce gave the free tickets too," Danika said as she looked out at her.

"When we sing 'True Love,' can you give her a shout-out. Her name is Brittney."

"Sure thing," Danika said, joining the rest of the band onstage as the song began.

***

(*Danika sings, metal sound.*)
'Twas the night before
A battle for the world
No words, just demons crying
I rode the wildfire
'Twas a blazing pyre
Now that our worlds collide
You think you found the answer
For I'm the necromancer
Forget the poetry
The cancer's in the world
Now we're living in desperate times

(Danika sings the chorus, metal sound.)
I've got a voice that will never fade
I've got the dreams and innocence of every man
You'll see me soaring across the blue, blue sky
You'll dream of me beneath the moonlit sky
I've got a story that you need to read
I am the memory that you hold deep

(Danika sings, metal sound.)
Returning from that journey
An unknown destination
I'm the tale they've read to you
When it starts the night
I'll battle the jinn and hellfire
I'll banish them to the depths of hell
A man's imagination
It's a dream emporium
Just think of all the tales they've read you
It's the story you can't escape
While you intoxicate
The cold thought of just living in desperate times

(Danika sings the chorus again, metal sound.)
I've got a voice that will never fade
I am the dreams and innocence of every man
You'll see me soaring across the blue, blue sky
You'll dream of me beneath the moonlit sky
I've become the story that you need to read
I've become every memory that you hold deep

(Danika sings, operatic/instrumental.)
Forever
The voice
That will never fade
Innocence
Of this world
Dream of me
Innocence
Of this world

(Danika sings, metal sound.)
I've got a voice that will never fade
With the dreams and innocence of every man
You see me soar through the blue, blue sky
Breaking through your moonlit sky
I am the story that you need to read
I am the memory that you hold deep . . .

(Music fades out slowly.)

***

"So we thought we'd slow it down a little, and what better way to slow it down than with 'True Love.' But in order to do that, I am going to need the help of my very beautiful girlfriend, Valerie Hammond!" Danika shouted, presenting me to the crowd, and they went wild as I walked onstage. "A big welcome to my girl Brittney up front here, we're so glad you made it."

"I need to come up there!" Brittney shouted.

"You need to come up here?" Danika repeated and smiled. "Well, I guess you should then," Danika said, as security escorted her on stage.

"So how are you, Brittney?" Danika asked and smiled and laughed with Brittney.

"I'm good. These are for you," Brittney said, handing Danika the red roses she was holding.

"Well, thank you," Danika said, giving Brittney a hug and accepting the flowers.

"You're welcome. Only they're not from me," Brittney said.

"Not from you?" Danika asked and smiled. "Who are they from then?"

"They're from Valerie," Brittney said, pointing at me.

When Danika turned around, she saw me on one knee with the most beautiful ring I had picked out from Ultra Diamonds.

"The most beautiful ring for the most beautiful woman in the world," I said and smiled as the crowd chanted, "Yes."

"Danika, will you marry me?" I asked her, speaking into the mic.

"That's funny that you ask," Danika said as she herself

pulled out a ring. "I was going to ask you the same question after we sang 'True Love' together."

And she and I joined hands and told each other, "Yes," with the music playing softly in the background. When we parted hands, I walked over to my cello and began playing softly. Brittney was escorted back to her seat in the front row after hugging us both.

****

(Danika sings in soft melody.)
Lie awake
Watching you sleep and dream
I pull you close and breathe you deep
Your smile stretches from cheek to cheek
Your face so perfect and sweet
I know loving you was my lifelong dream
The love we share is so true and deep
Together as one, apart as two
Our love has to be true

(Danika and Valerie sing together in soft melody.)
The love we share
Forever and true
Whatever the endeavor
Together we'll see it through
We are together forever in our love that's true
So please, let's make our love true

(Valerie sings in soft melody.)
I've been awake
Lying here watching you watch me
I pull you close and breathe you deep
In your dreams, those loving dreams
So real and true
Is where I'll lie and wait for you
Loving you has been my dream come true
Apart we're two
Until you found me and I found you
Together as one, where once there were two
Our love is true

(Danika and Valerie sing together in soft melody.)
The love we share
Forever and true
Whatever the endeavor
Together we'll see it through
We are together forever in a love that's true
Now I know, our love is true

(Song fades.)

***

Danika

When the concert ended, we jumped onto our private jet to leave Las Vegas and return home.

"This is the greatest day of my life," I said, touching Valerie's face and looking into her eyes before we shared another kiss.

"I'm so happy I have you. I love you so much," Valerie said. "What do you say, when we get home, I'll run down to the corner market and get us a bottle of champagne and we can take a bath?"

"That sounds wonderful. I'll pick some red roses from the garden while you're gone and draw us a bath."

When we got home, Valerie quickly left and headed to the store while I picked roses from the garden. After picking the petals off and spreading them into the bath and adding bubbles to the water, I got undressed and got into the tub. The warm water felt wonderful as it touched my naked body. After lying there for a few minutes, I picked up one of the rose stems and pricked my finger on one of the thorns. At that moment I saw a terrible premonition of Valerie dying in my arms.

I quickly jumped from the bath and flicked my wrist. As soon as the Nexus appeared and I was covered in my angelic armor, immediately jinn and reapers broke through the doors and windows of the house. They came at me like a rampant horde. I threw many of them off as if they were rag dolls. When a horde of them jumped on me and tried to tackle me to the ground, I put my fist to the ground and shot off like a rocket to the sky and they flew off me like dead leaves.

When I saw the market it looked over run with jinn and reapers. I came shooting down from the sky like a bullet, bursting through the ceiling landing in the frozen food section. I saw jinn and reapers everywhere. Walking up to a reaper who was about to kill a man. I drove the Nexus through it and it vanished.

"Thank you," the man said scared, "thank you so much," he said running off.

Killing every evil foe in my path. I saw Valerie.

"Valerie!" I shouted.

"Danika," she said when a black entity came up behind her and she turned around.

Reaching out the entity pulled her in close, pressing its hand to her stomach, it flicked its wrist. I saw a lightning bolt weapon pierce through her.

"Valerie!" I cried in horror as the entity let out a shriek, and all the jinn and reapers vanished to thin air.

"Danika, Danika . . . ," I heard Valerie say in a shallow voice. She was spitting up blood.

"Don't talk, baby," I said as I rushed to her side. "Tigist, it was Dean."

You don't know that, Tigist said.

"Who else has a lightning bolt spear for a weapon?" I said calm trying not to cry. "I should have let him die when he fell from that roof."

Picking Valerie's head up, I placed it on my thighs and sat with her.

"It's okay," Valerie said, breathing shallow. She began to cry.

"Please don't try to talk, baby. Tigist, we have to help her, please!" I said sobbing. "Tell me what to do?" I cried.

"It's okay, Danika," Valerie said again as she gasped for air and tears rolled down her cheeks.

"Tigist! Help me!" I said panicking as we tried combining our powers to help Valerie. "Why isn't it working?" I said, panicking even more. "I can't do this without you, Valerie. Please don't leave me."

"Danika, baby, it's okay," Valerie said calmly. Her face turning pale.

"It's not okay," I said, crying and wiping my tears taking deep breaths.

"It is though," Valerie said, taking a deep breath. "I got to have you," Valerie said, taking a deep breath as her bottom lip trembled. "I need you to be strong."

"I don't want to," I said as Valerie softly closed her eyes. "I don't want to do any of this without you," I said cutting my hand and when the blood came I put it in her wound.

"Why is nothing working?"

"Because I'm not supposed to survive this," Valerie said breathing deep. "I'm so scared Danika," Valerie said. "Will you kiss me? I want to breath my last breath into you. I'm cold," she said shivering as I put my lips to hers. "I'm so cold," she whispered before taking her last breath.

The Tainted Angel

Jensen

With Valerie's death came, a dark, turbulent cloud that settled over Danika. She secluded herself to her home and refused to see or talk to anyone. She became a ghost, an empty shell of her former self. This was also the time that Maya came back into her life to try and help ease the pain. But she didn't care about anything anymore. She blamed herself for what happened to Valerie.

I had seen the news reports of what journalists and news anchors called an angelic vigilante. Photographs of this vigilante had been taken everywhere around the world, but none had captured a positive ID of what the vigilante looked like. What they did know was that she appeared to be a woman in her late teens or early twenties. She had stopped countless crimes across the globe and had gotten American troops out of harm's way in the Middle East as some terror groups were still at large after Majid El-Khatib's mission of peace. Bad guys around the world had all been running scared ever since the rise of this angelic vigilante. I knew the vigilante was Danika when I saw one of the pictures and I could see the single dutch french braid she favors.

Pulling up to Danika's house, I parked and rang the doorbell when I noticed the front door was ajar. Opening the door slowly, I walked inside. I looked around, and I saw that the plants in the atrium had all died. Everything was covered in dust, as if no one really lived in this once-beautiful place. It looked as if it was condemned doors were broken off the hinges. All the windows were broken. Opening the refrigerator, I noticed that everything in there was out of date or covered in mold. The only things that were still in perfect condition throughout the house were all the pictures of Danika and Valerie together or of just Valerie alone. There was one picture in particular that I could tell was favored in this sad place. It was a candid eight-by-ten photo of Valerie gently resting her forehead on Danika's; they were ever so slightly smiling at each other. It was an absolutely beautiful picture of the both of them in a more blissful time. I could tell this picture of them was taken at the beach as I could see they were both in bikini bathing suits and their surfboards were in the background. Taking me out of my reverie, suddenly I felt a cold breeze. Looking out into the atrium, I saw Danika.

"Where have you been?" I asked, still holding the picture.

"Does it matter?" Danika said coldly. "What are you doing here?" she asked, walking past me.

"I wanted to check on you," I said.

"Well, you checked," Danika responded. "Now go."

"Do you think Valerie would want to see you like this?" I asked.

"What the hell do you know?" Danika shouted, flicking her wrist and swinging the Nexus at me.

"More than you think," I said calmly, dodging the Nexus.

After many initial attempts of her trying to hit me, I dodged them all till she finally stopped.

"I won't fight you, Danika," I said.

"Just leave," Danika said, becoming emotional as she squinted her eyes, trying not to cry.

"There's nothing I can say to you to make things different. I can't bring Valerie back, but you can," I said.

"How do I do that?" Danika asked.

"Believe in yourself the way I believe in you," I said, looking at her. "Love yourself again."

"I can't do that," she said looking at me. "Do you know what this is?" Danika said, flicking her wrist, then a Trivium blade appeared.

"Where did you get that?" I asked.

"It doesn't matter," Danika said. "My heart is completely broken. Everything I do reminds me of Valerie. I'll never get over this," Danika said sobbing. "I want you to go," Danika said, fighting back tears again before picking up a dead rose from the garden and holding it. I watched as the rose came back to life in her hands.

"Danika," I said.

"Leave, Dad!" she shouted in anger. "Go!"

"I love you," I said before walking out the door.

Anonymous Angel

Opening the front door, I walked into Jensen's home. I saw happiness in the pictures everywhere I looked. When I saw a picture of Nathaniel and Maya together, I picked it up and looked closely at it. Thinking about how far I'd come since the day heaven fell to chaos, I looked at the picture and touched Nathaniel's face.

"I love you, Nathaniel," I said, still touching his face in the picture with my thumb.

Suddenly I heard a beep from a car door locking. Looking out the window, I saw Maya walking up the pathway to the front door. I quickly hid in a coat closet nearby. When I heard the front door open, I felt rage come over me. Taking a deep breath, I closed my eyes and meditated. When I heard her climbing up the stairs, I stepped out of the closet, and I felt the tip of a katana being held to my back.

"I knew you'd come, Everin," Maya said, staying alert.

"How's that?" I asked.

"Your daughter sold you out," Maya said.

"You lie," I said.

"I won't lie. It took a bit of convincing, but then Rayne understood," Maya said.

Quickly I flicked my wrist, and when my lightning bolt sword appeared, I hit Maya's katana away from my shoulder in one smooth motion.

"You'd think that after everything I've done for you, you'd just be loyal. But even after I saved you from that pig, Roquin, oh . . . how you resisted me, and the more you resisted, the more I wanted you," Maya said in a seductive tone. "How did you break free of my grasp anyway?" Maya asked.

"Why do you ask questions to which you already know the answer?" I asked.

"You're right. I do know the answer to that question, and Dean has proven to be quite menacing. But he'll be dealt with soon enough," Maya said.

"You should be ashamed of yourself," I said.

"Come now, Everin. You don't miss it, the things the abyss had to teach? Nathaniel, Roquin, you, and I were students to its lessons. We learned many great things. Nathaniel understood the powers of the abyss all too well, as I did," Maya said. "He probably would've joined me if I asked him to," Maya said, deep in thought.

"Nathaniel would've never joined you," I said, taking a swing at Maya as she dodged it.

"Don't be so sure about that," Maya said. "He saw the flaws in God's system, as we all did," Maya said. "I was just the only one with enough courage to stand up and point them out."

"This is your idea of pointing out flaws?" I asked shocked.

"You call it what you want," Maya said firmly. "God is dead, and I'm the new supreme being!"

"And what of Danika?" I asked.

"Well, let's just say, we won't have to deal with that beautiful disaster much longer," Maya said. "I took from her the one thing that meant everything, and pretty soon she won't be a thorn in my side. She now has everything she needs to destroy herself."

"If you're so powerful. Why wouldn't you of destroyed her long ago?"

"I still have a heart. Despite what you may think. I wanted her join me," Maya said remorseful. "I couldn't kill her."

"So have her do it. So her death isn't on your conscience. That's why you gave her a Trivium blade," I said.

"Yes," Maya said.

"You'll tell my family the truth about everything, or so help me, Maya," I said, threatening her.

"What makes you think I'd do that? Jensen's my son. What makes you think he'd ever betray me, for you? Who do you think taught him everything he knows? Who do you think has been there since day one, nurturing him, guiding him, manipulating him? I've groomed him and Rayne both, and they are loyal to me. When they say 'Mother,' it's my face they see," Maya said sinisterly. "Both your children are mine," she continued. "Face it,

Everin, I've been here since the beginning, and I'll be here at the end," Maya ended before we heard a door upstairs open.

"Showtime," Maya said as she cut her own arm with her katana and fell to the floor. "Jensen . . . ," Maya said with a whimper, "she's trying to kill me. She's the one that murdered Valerie, and now she's trying to murder me."

"Jensen, don't believe her," I begged as Jensen flicked his wrist. "Please, son, you must believe me," I said as Jensen looked at Maya.

"First, don't ever call me son again," Jensen said, pointing the Nevillin at Maya. "Second, my father was the one who was there from day one, not you. He nurtured me, he guided me, he loved me, but never did he manipulate me," Jensen said, looking at Maya. "You look confused," Jensen continued. "I bet you're wondering how I came to know these things. Allow me to answer that question for you," Jensen said when Dean walked into the room.

"I should have known," Maya said, looking at Dean.

"Yeah, you probably should have," Dean said. "You'd think, you'd have learned by now that I'm a bad penny, a thorn on the side, a monkey with a wrench."

"Well, none of you are strong enough to defeat me. You know it, and I know it. So who wants to die first?" Maya asked when all of a sudden her clothes changed to dark angelic armor and she flicked her wrist and her katana appeared.

"Danika's in danger, Jensen, you must get to her!" Everin shouted, as Maya swung her katana and Everin in one swift motion flicked her wrist and when her lightening bolt sword appeared she blocked Maya's attack. "I'll keep Maya here."

"You're already too late," Maya said.

"What does she mean, Danika is in danger?" Dean asked, looking at me as we ran out the door and jumped in my truck.

"I don't know," I responded as we sped off.

We tried several times to call Danika, but every time, her phone just rang and rang without any answer.

"Man, I hope Everin's going to be okay," Dean said sadly.

***

Danika

I'd taken the rose I was holding and laid it on the corner of the tub. I lit candles around the bathtub and turned the water on. Flicking my wrist, I placed the Trivium blade next to the rose. Taking a deep breath, I began to cry. I flicked my wrist a third time, and the elder grimoire appeared.

Please, Danika, don't do this, Tigist pleaded. *I beg you.*

"It's over, Tigist," I said, looking at her.

If you kill yourself, you kill us, Tigist said scared. *You kill me.*

Opening the elder grimoire to a blank page, I stared at it. I always wondered what my first entry in the grimoire would be. I'd never thought my first would be my last. Thinking about Valerie, I cried, and as my tears hit the blank pages of the grimoire, words began to appear as Tigist flew out of a nearby window.

To whom it may concern:

My name is Danika. If you're reading this, it means that I'm dead and no longer a burden to this world. To better understand how I came to the decision of taking my own life, I would need to tell you about how I came to be in the dark place where I am now. I thought it would be fitting to write this short chapter of my life in the elder grimoire as it's the book that chronicles my family's origin.

I was born in Dana Point, California. I don't remember much of those early years, but I do remember often gazing at the clouds and wondering if Godric was still up there. My mother had a successful career in the music industry and became quite an icon. She was revered by many for being an extreme philanthropist. It wasn't until I was born that she fell into a coma, only to never wake up. When I was thirteen, I found myself attracted to a girl named Ruth. I remember questioning my thoughts, but the way the sun touched her hair, I had never seen someone so beautiful. I thought we'd love each other forever. I remember our teacher telling us it was just an adolescent phase and that we'd outgrow it. Ruth did; I didn't.

When I met Valerie, it was as if time stopped and everything stood still. It was in my high school music class. I was aspiring to become as great a singer as my mother. Valerie played the cello. I could listen to her play for hours. I could hear every note. The first time we kissed, I knew I never wanted to kiss anyone but her again. She became my everything. This was also the time I came out to my father. He was accepting of my choices and supported my actions. Valerie's parents repudiated her and made her feel ashamed. Much like Valerie's, parents there were people in my life who hated my decisions and always reminded me of it .

I had always known what I wanted to do with my life. I reformed my parents' legendary symphonic metal band, Embrace the Fate, with myself taking over the lead vocals. It was a beautiful time in my life where everything was falling into place, and I was so happy I had Valerie to spend my life with. Our love story was embedded in the house we bought together in the Nigel Shores, which overlooked the beautiful ocean. We'd surf every day and work in our atrium where we grew roses, jasmines, and gardenias, and our place always smelled beautiful.

But as fate would have it, all I have now are blissful memories of a life that was taken from me. It happened a year ago. In an instant, my life changed forever, and she was gone, taken from me. I never cried so hard in my life. After this, our once-beautiful home became as I am now: dead inside, broken, and empty. I've isolated myself from everyone and everything and apologized for nothing. It seems strange that my life should end this way. But for all the years I had with Valerie, all I knew was love and happiness.

I shall die here now, alone, broken, and empty. Never fearing, never forgiving, and never forgetting. Everything I once was is gone now in the blink of an eye. Everything I believed in perished. I'm broken and lost without my Valerie. I leave this place of my own free will, with no apologies.

—Danika

Taking my clothes off after the grimoire recorded my entry, I stepped into the bathtub. I heard the sound of tires skidding across the pavement outside.

***

Jensen

Jensen, you have to get in there. Danika is about to do something terrible, Tigist said, flying up to me outside as I ran to the door.

Danika

I slowly inserted the Trivium blade into my right wrist. When the incision was made, the Trivium blade disappeared. The rain continued to pour down, and the thunder and lightning clashed and roared.

Jensen

"Tigist, are you okay?" Dean asked, catching her as she fell from midair.

Danika

Holding my hand to my left wrist, I flicked it, and the Nexus pierced straight through and disappeared.

Dean

Dean, it's too late for me, Tigist said in a shallow breath.

Taking a knee in Danika's house, Dean laid Tigist down on the floor as I ran upstairs to get to her, and the whole house began to shake. Looking at Tigist, Dean watched as she closed her eyes and disappeared.

Jensen

"Danika!" I shouted. "Where are you?"

When I heard water running in the bathroom and saw water all over the floor coming from under the bathroom door, I kicked the door open. Feeling uneasy and scared, I struggled to see through the steam. I looked around, and there in the bathtub was Danika's lifeless body. In her left hand she was holding a wilting rose. The water and blood flowed together as I lifted her from the bath, panicking and in fear I held her close and sat on the floor.

"What did you do, baby?" I said sobbing as Dean ran in.

"Daddy," Danika said, crying and trying to lift her hand and touch my face, "I'm sorry."

"Baby, don't talk," I said, shaking and panicking.

"I failed," she said. "I failed you. I failed Valerie."

"I love you, Danika," I told her as she closed her eyes and the dying rose fell from her hand.

Still holding her close I cried as her body slowly disappeared. I felt an uncontrollable rage come over me.

"I'm so sorry, Jensen," Everin said, walking into the bathroom behind Dean.

"Where's Maya?" I asked.

"She fled," Everin said, walking over to the window in Danika's bedroom.

"I'm gonna kill her," I said distraught.

"I'm going to help you," Dean said sadly.

"The only one that has the power to kill her is Danika," Everin said.

"Then I'll die trying," I said, crying harder now.

"You know me, brother," Dean said, giving me a hug. "I'm with you till the end,"

"We must cling to hope," Everin said.

Dean

Walking to the window, the three of us looked and saw that the lightning had caused numerous fires. With the TV on in the background, we heard that chaos was all around us now and that the new temple Majid El-Khatib had built was now in ruins as Maya's army of evil fell from the sky and embedded themselves everywhere around the world. I took the framed blissful, candid eight-by-ten photo of Valerie gently resting her forehead on Danika's and gave it to Jensen.

"Why are you giving me this?" Jensen asked, trying to hold back his tears now.

"Because Danika's going to want this when she returns," I said firmly, staying strong for Jensen.

The End

About the Author

Timothy Aberle was born in Las Vegas, Nevada. At the age of eight, his family migrated to Dana Point, California. Growing up with two brothers, he learned the importance of friendship and loyalty. Regularly attending Saint Edwards Catholic Church with his family, he developed a strong interest in religion and decided to research as many different religions as possible throughout his years.

Having an eccentric imagination, he drew inspiration through different genres of music and adventurous movies. Growing up on the beaches of Strands and Salt Creek, he grew a deep respect and love for the ocean. His love for the ocean fueled his imagination and daydreaming about the unknown became normal. While others found surfing and boogie boarding to be great pastimes, Timothy often wrote short stories and songs in a journal and spent much of his time at the local library reading Stephen King books. It wasn't till he attended Dana Hills High School that Timothy enrolled himself in a bible literature class in search of further educating himself on religion. At this time, he penned a short story called Cain's Fury as a project for class and received high praise for its creativity.

A big turning point in Timothy's life was when his mother, Donna, fell ill to a rare deadly disease called scleroderma. His mother stricken with grief, desperately turned to reading inspirational books about Angels to help cope with the stress of being sick. Through chemotherapy and heart wrenching times, Timothy witnessed the courage of both his mother and father. On October 3rd, 1999 tragedy fell over Timothy's household when his beloved mother, Donna, passed away.

Moving back to Las Vegas to start over, Timothy fell in love with a young lady with a love for books. After sharing his short story, Cain's Fury, with the young lady who he would soon marry, she encouraged him to allow his imagination to go to work and he began writing his debut novel. Using Cain's Fury as the template, **Chronicles of Kane** was born.

Timothy resides in Las Vegas with his wife and two children, Dean and Sam. He works for a luxury home builder as a customer care representative and remains hard at work on **Supremacy of Kane**, the last volume in the Kane trilogy.

Book One: Chronicles of Kane

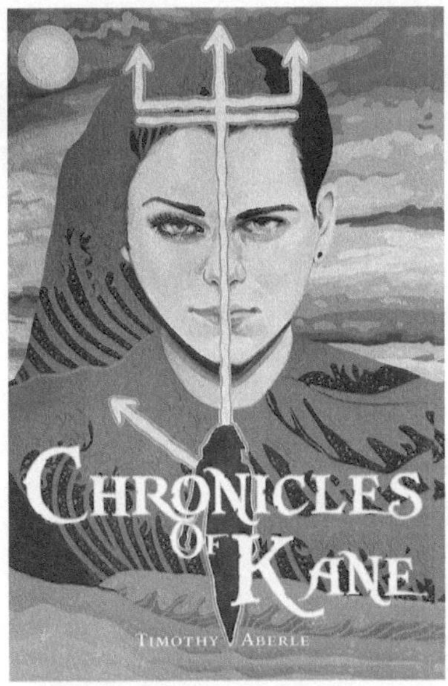

ISBN: 978-1-941049-03-7

www.ingramcontent.com/pod-product-compliance
Lightning Source LLC
Chambersburg PA
CBHW020807190726
48285CB00006B/2186